## THE HORRORS OF WAR . . .

"Colonel Mot, the Saigon government will never win the support of the people in this way," Ernie said.

Mot laughed a short, cryptic laugh. "We don't need their support, Mr. Chapel," he said, taking in the people of the market with a wave of his hand. "All we need is their fear. And for that, there is nothing better than a public execution."

The guards moved the four men into position against the wall of one of the nearby buildings. The bolt on the Jeep-mounted machine gun was slammed home.

While Ernie watched in disbelief and horror, the gun opened up, not popping like a small gun, but exploding in earth-shaking, stomach-jarring blasts.

The little men began to fly apart. Arms and legs were literally shredded. One of them was completely cut in half. The top of his body toppled over backward, and the bottom half stood for a moment gushing blood, then fell forward.

Suddenly the gun stopped, and the relative silence of the bickering Vietnamese again filled the air. Only the children watched; the vendors and the buyers seemed oblivious to the killings.

## DATELINE: PHU LOI

# DATELINE: PHU LOI

**Ernie Chapel**

*PaperJacks* LTD.

TORONTO    NEW YORK

AN ORIGINAL

*PaperJacks*

## DATELINE: PHU LOI

*PaperJacks* LTD

330 STEELCASE RD. E., MARKHAM, ONT. L3R 2M1
210 FIFTH AVE., NEW YORK, N.Y. 10010

PaperJacks edition published October 1987

ISBN 0-7701-0644-7
Printed in the USA

# DATELINE: PHU LOI

# Prologue

**WASHINGTON
SPRING, 1986**

"You're sure you don't want a retirement banquet? The White House press secretary said he would be glad to be our dinner speaker."

Ernie Chapel was standing at the window of the Washington bureau of Combined Press International, looking out toward the Jefferson Memorial. He brushed a hand through hair that he continued to describe as brindle, even though it was now white. His eyes were blue and his face was more weathered than wrinkled. He was wearing jeans and an old army field jacket.

He turned away from the window to look at Carl Walters, the Washington bureau chief. In his younger days as an activist, Carl had stormed the barricades on college campuses, marched in the streets of New York and Washington, and smelled the tear gas in Chicago during the '68 Democratic convention. Now he was a clean-shaven, well-dressed, conservative, upwardly mobile pillar of society. The caterpillar had turned into a butterfly.

"No doubt the press secretary would have a few well-chosen words about the nobleness of our profession, about how freedom of the press is one of the most fundamental rights we have, how we must guard it, that sort of thing?" Ernie asked.

"They are words we live by," Carl said. "You have been a professional journalist for over forty years. Surely they mean something to you?"

Ernie chuckled. "Oh, yes, they're important to me. But it has always been my impression that the louder the horn is tooted, the less meaning the words have."

"What do you mean?"

Ernie pointed toward the Jefferson Memorial. "Did you know that Jefferson said, 'Given the opportunity to live in a nation without a government, or a nation without a newspaper, I would chose a nation without a government'?"

"Of course. Everyone knows that," Carl said. "It's on the masthead of hundreds of newspapers."

"Ah, yes, so it is. But this same champion of the press also said, 'Truth itself is polluted when printed in a newspaper.' How many mastheads will you find that on?"

"Not many, I suppose," Carl admitted.

"No, I guess not," Ernie said. He looked at the gold watch Carl had just given him.

> For 42 years of faithful service to the sacred
> fourth estate.
> Ernest R. Chapel
> journalist
> 1944–1986
> Combined Press International

"Pretty," he said. He slipped it on his wrist. "Always wanted a Rolex."

"We're going to miss you around here, Ernie," Carl said.

Ernie looked through the glass window of Carl's office out onto the floor at the dozen desks of the Washington staff. Phones were ringing, computer printouts were tapping, monitors were blinking.

"You won't miss me," Ernie said. "You have visual display terminals, telephone modems, and hardcopy printouts. What the hell do you need with a broken-down old pencil pusher?"

"You know how to put heart in a story," Carl said simply. "That's something you can't get from a VDT."

Ernie smiled. "Carl, my boy, there may be hope for you yet." He started toward the door.

"This is it? No ceremony of any kind?" Carl asked.

Ernie tapped his gold watch. "This and my retirement check," he said, "is all the ceremony I need."

"Where are you going now?"

"Now?" Ernie replied. He stroked his jaw thoughtfully. "Now, I'm going to say good-bye to a lot of friends."

"Anyone I know?"

"No," Ernie said. "I don't think so."

Ernie Chapel stood at the head of the incline and stared down at the shining black granite memorial. The wall reflected the solemn faces of the veterans and of their families as they walked slowly along its length, stopping here and there to reach out and touch a name. The lips of some of the men moved softly, and occasionally Ernie could overhear one of them.

"Ole Terry, he always was good for a beer."

Or: "That dumb-assed Kincaid never did learn to keep his mouth shut. He was always talkin' back to somebody, always in trouble." A pause. "I guess it's shut now, though."

The visitors talked only as they were going down, or coming back up, the incline. While they were actually in front of the names they listened with their hearts to the silent voices of the 58,022 who died in Vietnam.

Ernie stood there for half an hour, trying to get up the nerve to go down . . . to descend into that valley of death and to commune with those whose stories he had told during the long, bitter war.

Ernie had seen the war from the beginning to the end as a correspondent for CPI. He saw it all, from the bloody booby traps on the My Kahn Floating Restaurant in Saigon, to the human-wave attacks at Khesahn. He had drunk champagne with fat corrupt Vietnamese generals in the eighth-floor bar of the Hotel Caravel . . . and shared tepid canteen water with American grunts in the Iron Triangle. He had fondled the breasts of lovely young girls on the beaches at Vung Tau, and once he had held the hand of a black American soldier as he watched life leave his eyes.

Ernie reported on what he saw in weekly — sometimes daily — dispatches for his news bureau. He had been there even before the American involvement when the great combat photographer, Bob Capa, was killed. He was there with Pulitzer Prize-winner David Halberstam when the protesting monks were setting themselves on fire, and when Diem and his brother were killed. He had eaten dinner with the French writer Bernard Fall on the night before Fall took his final ride in the back seat of a fighter-bomber. His death hushed one of the Vietnam War's most knowledgeable voices.

Ernie had cried with his fellow journalists when the much beloved woman reporter Dickie Chappelle was killed by a Claymore mine while doing the photo article of a marine patrol for *National Geographic* magazine.

But Ernie was retired now, pensioned off with a gold watch and his memories. His time was his own. He could buy the boat he always wanted or finish the novel he had started twenty years ago.

Or, he could write the stories, the real stories that, for one reason or another, had been left untold.

Ernie put his hand on the shining black monument. "I owe all of you an apology," he said quietly. "Sometimes deadlines, censors, and sensibilities got in the way of the truth and I didn't always tell the whole story.''

He took a deep breath and let out a sigh as he suddenly realized what he would do with all the free time that was now his. The boat and the novel could wait.

"But, by God, I will write the story now," he said softly.

# Chapter One

AIR ASSAULT TROOPS IN ACTION IN VIETNAM
AGAINST ENEMY

by Ernie Chapel

PHU LOI, March 15, 1968 (CPI) — The
United States and South Vietnamese military
commands have launched a major air assault
in the rich rice-producing area of central Vietnam. The attack is an effort to trap and
destroy units of enemy regiments who are
operating there.

The assault involves more than 10,000
American and South Vietnamese troops, including air force, artillery, and armor-support
elements.

The assault elements are transported to designated areas, known as "landing zones" or LZ's, by UH-1 "Huey" helicopters. There, the troops leap off the helicopters, sometimes even before they touch the ground, as they rush into the attack.

The transport helicopters are escorted by armed Hueys, officially called "UH-1C gunships," though referred to by the troops as "hogs," because the externally attached machine gun and rocket launchers which give the helicopters a deadly punch also make them slow and awkward.

Just how slow and how awkward is best understood when riding inside a hog as you watch tracer rounds coming toward you. This reporter was recently afforded that opportunity.

A large "V" of helicopters lifted off the perforated steel planking. Then, climbing and accelerating, they swung left. Their departure path took them over Tent City, several rows of neatly aligned tents. The angry growl of a dozen turbine engines and the popping of the whirling rotor blades caused a surf of sound to wash over the tents, then roll along the ground, following the Hueys as they headed north from the sprawling helicopter base.

Ernie Chapel, a war correspondent for Combined Press International, had made arrangements to go along on this mission, but his Jeep ride up from Saigon was delayed by roadblocks. Now it was too late. The mission was under way and he was on the ground.

The departing helicopters passed over the officers' shower, where the lone occupant looked up. Chief Warrant Officer Mike Carmack had soap lather on his neck and shoulders, under his arms, and between his legs. He reached up to pull the rope that would open the valve to allow water to drain from the fifty-five-gallon drum. Instead of being rewarded with a steady gush of water, however, he received only a frustrating trickle.

"Son of a bitch!" he shouted. He could feel the soap beginning to dry, and his skin, already blistered into a rash from half a dozen jungle maladies, started to itch.

Mike stepped out from behind the canvas baffles of the jury-rigged shower and looked out over the company area for SP-5 Schuler, the NCOIC of the mama-san workers. It was Schuler's responsibility to make certain that his women kept the water tanks over the showers full, and the honey buckets under the latrines empty.

"Schuler!" Mike bellowed, and a dozen busy mama-sans looked over at him and saw him standing there, nude except for the patches of lather that flocked his skin. They put their hands to their mouths and laughed. "Schuler, where the hell are you?" Mike called, totally oblivious to the reaction of the mama-sans.

SP-5 Schuler came running around the corner of the C.P. tent to answer Mike's call.

"I'm right here, Mr. Carmack! What is it? What's wrong?"

"Water, Schuler," Mike said, pointing to the empty drums over the shower. "It's very difficult to take a shower without water."

"I'm sorry, sir. Colonel Todaro wanted his shower filled first."

"What the hell for? He wasn't on duty all night. I was."

"I know, sir, but he's the colonel."

"Did you fill his?"

"Yes, sir."

"Good," Mike said. He stepped behind the canvas baffles of the officers' shower, then reappeared a moment later holding his change of clothes and towel. Then, with his shower clogs flapping noisily, he walked across the quadrangle toward the small, one-man shower that the battalion commander had ordered built for himself.

"Oh, no, Mr. Carmack, you can't do that!" Schuler shouted when he saw where Mike was headed. "Mr. Carmack, you don't want to use the colonel's shower, sir! He'll have your ass!"

"At least it'll be a clean ass," Mike called back over his shoulder.

Colonel Todaro's shower was constructed of plywood, lined inside with shining sheets of aluminum. The aluminum was pilfered from maintenance. The fact that there were half a dozen bullet-punctured helicopters that needed the sheet metal for skin patches didn't delay the construction.

Colonel Todaro had spigots to control his water. The water came from two tanks, one painted black to allow the sun to heat the water, and the other white, to keep the water cool. By mixing the water from the two tanks, one could have a shower of perfect temperature.

Mike rinsed himself off. Then, because he was enjoying the colonel's shower so much, he lathered up and rinsed again. As he was drying off, he noticed that the colonel had a bottle of men's cologne, so he made generous use of it. Then, with a towel tied around his waist to restore some modesty, he strolled leisurely back to his tent. He didn't have to report to work until 1400, and he intended to take maximum advantage of the morning off.

Ernie had watched the entire exchange. He could smell the cologne as Mike passed close by. He chuckled.

"Enjoy your shower, Chief?" he asked as Mike started toward his tent.

"Who are you?"

Ernie smiled and stuck out his hand. "Ernie Chapel, CPI."

"I'm Mike Carmack. CPI? You a newspaper reporter?"

"Yes. Why? Are you against reporters?"

"No, not if you're with the newspapers," Mike said. "It's the TV guys give me a pain in the ass. I've seen them fake enough stories to make a goddamned movie. What you doin' here?"

"I was supposed to go along on the lift this morning, but I didn't make it up from Saigon in time. I was held up by a roadblock in Phu Cuong."

"You didn't miss anything," Mike said. "It's a soft LZ this morning."

"Those are the kind I like," Ernie said.

Mike raised his eyebrows. "Oh? Where's the old 'into the heat of battle' urge I thought all reporters had?"

"The only urge I have is to stay alive," Ernie said.

Mike laughed. "You're okay," he said. "I'm sorry you were too late. Listen, you want a Coke? I've got some in here. They aren't cold but they're wet."

"Don't mind if I do," Ernie answered.

Ernie didn't know why he looked back at the lone, returning helicopter. There was really nothing different about the sound . . . and yet, there must have been, because even before he looked around, he had a feeling of apprehension.

"Mike," he said in a strained voice, "look."

The Huey was coming in low, no more than a hundred feet above the ground, and it was flying at a severe crab to keep the fire out of the cockpit and cabin. Flames streamed away from the helicopter, blue and white in close to the fuselage, orange a little farther out. From there it turned into a thick, black smoke. As Ernie and Mike watched the helicopter approach, they saw the door gunner crawling out onto the skid and they knew he was about to jump.

"No!" Mike shouted, even though he knew it was impossible for the door gunner to hear him. "You're too high!"

The door gunner jumped despite Mike's warning. He hadn't disconnected his APH-5 helmet, and the long mike cord streamed out behind him like the static line on a parachute. When the gunner reached the end of the cord, the cord jerked his helmet off his head, while the door gunner, his arms flailing ineffectively at the air, fell nearly one hundred feet.

Ernie saw a little puff of dust rise from where the gunner hit. He felt a sickening sensation in his stomach. Then he turned to watch the helicopter as it approached the airfield. The pilot managed to clear Tent City, but he didn't even attempt to make it all the way over to the perforated steel planking. Instead, he set it down in the very first clearing beyond the tents.

It didn't work. The slipstream had been keeping the flames away, but as soon as the pilot set it down he lost the slipstream effect and the fire was sucked back into the fuel cells. The tanks exploded in a great, greasy ball of fire.

No one got out.

"Son of a bitch," Mike said softly, and it was more of a prayer than an oath.

Ernie leaned back against the stack of sandbags that surrounded the tent. He felt nauseous, and he broke out in a sweat. He was still standing there a moment later when the med-evac helicopter landed near where the door gunner had fallen. He watched the medics lift the still form of the gunner into the chopper. Then the chopper lifted off and, nose down, started toward the First Field hospital in Saigon, twenty minutes away.

Mike went into his tent and lay down on his bunk. Ernie followed him inside and sat on a chair near the table in the middle of the floor.

"We have six people bunkin' in here," Mike said, as if answering a need to talk. "Four warrants and two lieutenants. The lieutenants are okay, though, so I don't mind them being here. My best friend, John Rindell, sleeps in the bunk next to mine." Mike sighed. "John and everyone else in here are on the mission you were supposed to go on."

Ernie knew that the helicopter that had just

crashed had been on the same mission. Who was it? Was it Mike's friend, John? It could have been. It didn't matter who it was now, because they were all dead.

Ernie looked up at the plethora of Playmate pictures that were tacked to the stained-plywood wall lockers. The beautiful girls — blondes, brunettes, and redheads — looked back at him with the same boobs and butts, and the same fixed smiles and blank eyes they had worn this morning. Smoke from the burning helicopter drifted through the tent, bringing with it the smell of the JP-4 fumes and the sickly sweet odor of burned flesh, but the expressions on the faces of the Playmates didn't change.

"Mr. Carmack?"

Ernie and Mike looked toward the end of the tent and saw Sergeant Pohl standing there. Ernie had spoken to Pohl just a few minutes earlier, so he recognized him as the operations sergeant.

"Yeah."

"I'm sorry, sir, but Cap'n Wilson has to get a reaction team up. The LZ is so hot they can't get the insertion in. The colonel wants ever' gun we got. We've only got four flyable right now, and not enough pilots unless we use you."

"All right," Mike said. He started getting dressed. "Who was it?" he asked.

"Mr. Bostic," Sergeant Pohl said. "Mr. Lumsden was flyin' with him. Windom was the crew chief."

"What about the door gunner?"

Sergeant Pohl shook his head. "He didn't make it. He died on the way to Saigon."

"Who was it?"

"It was Crowley."

"You knew him?" Ernie asked.

"I knew all of them. Hell, there's no one in the company I don't know. Mr. Lumsden was new, a W-1 right out of flight school. Bostic was a W-3 who'd been around a long time. I was on the bowling team with him in Germany."

"I'm sorry," Ernie said.

"That's the way it happens sometimes. Listen, you want to go with me?" Mike asked Ernie.

"Yeah, sure, if you don't mind," Ernie responded quickly.

"Get 'im a flak vest and a brain bucket," Mike told Sergeant Pohl. The brain bucket, Ernie knew, was a flight helmet.

Five minutes later Ernie was at the pad. The UH-1C model helicopter squatted there, waiting for him. The "hog" was bristling with weapons. On pylons to either side there were rocket tubes and, above each set of rocket tubes, one 7.62-mm machine gun. The machine gun was loaded with tracer ammunition and was used more for marking the target for the rockets than for the actual effect of the bullets.

Mounted guns stood in each door. Albritton, the door gunner, was making certain the weapons were ready, while Smith, the crew chief, who also manned one of the door guns during flight, had just untied the blade and was bringing it around. Mr. Dobbins was sitting in the left seat, the co-pilot's seat. He was already strapped in and going over the switches.

"We're carrying a passenger," Mike said as he slid back the "chicken plate," as the armored shield on his seat was called. "He's Ernie Chapel, a newspaper reporter."

"You can ride there, Mr. Chapel," Albritton invited, pointing to a forward-facing, red nylon jump seat that was right behind the two pilots.

"Thanks," Ernie said.

There were three other gunships here, and their crews were getting them ready as well. The flight leader would be Captain Bailey.

"Did you have time to pre-flight, Dob?" Mike asked his co-pilot.

"Yeah," Dobbins answered.

Smith waited until Mike was in his seat. Then he slid the chicken plate forward, so that Mike was sitting in, and wrapped with, armor plating. Mike put on his APH-5 and plugged in the cord, then flipped on the battery, the start-gen, and the aux fuel pump. He rolled up the throttle, then beeped down the auto fuel-control switch, and keyed the intercom. Ernie could hear the pre-start conversation through his own flight helmet.

"Smitty, you standing fireguard?"

"Yes, sir," Smitty answered. Smitty was standing outside the ship, but he had an extra-long mike cord that allowed him to move around while still being in contact with the rest of the crew.

"Clear," Mike said. He pulled the starter trigger, which was located under the collective, and Ernie could hear the snap of the igniters in his earphones as the turbine started turning over.

Mike monitored the N1 and N2 gauge, holding his hand over the starter switch, ready to abort if he got a hung or hot start. When it reached thirteen percent, he moved his hand away.

"Gunslinger Lead, this is Two," he called. "I have a good start."

"Three with a start."

"Four, I have a start."

"Flight up," Bailey said, and the four helicopters lifted off the pads, then queued out over Tent City and headed for the LZ.

The sky was such a brilliant blue that, even through the flight visor, Ernie had to squint. Below them rolled little shrub-covered hills and valleys of elephant grass. They passed over little villages that were no more than clusters of houses gathered at the edges of rice paddies.

Then, fifteen minutes later, Ernie saw Dobbins point out a dozen orbiting helicopters.

"Gunslinger Six, this is Gunslinger Lead. I have four hogs. Where do you want us?" Bailey called Gunslinger as the four gunships approached the LZ.

"Hello, Gunslinger Lead. This was supposed to be a soft LZ, but we took some pretty heavy fire from the trees near those three hootches down there. You think you can do something about it?"

"Roger," Gunslinger Lead answered.

Ernie looked down toward the trees Gunslinger Six had mentioned, and he saw that the hootches were right in the middle. It seemed impossible to fire into the trees without hitting the houses as well. Evidently Mike had the same thought.

"Gunslinger Lead, those hootches are right there," Mike said.

"Torch them," Gunslinger Lead said easily.

"Hey, Mike, what is that?" Dobbins asked, pointing to little black puffs that were erupting near them. Mike looked in the direction Dobbins pointed where a brilliant flash appeared, to be replaced immediately by one of the little black puffs.

"Air bursts!" Mike said. "Son of a bitch! We've got air bursts! Gunslinger Lead, do you observe alpha-alpha?"

"Affirmative," Gunslinger Lead answered. "We'll deploy in teams of two and approach the target on the deck."

Captain Bailey and three slot broke out, leaving Mike, who was in two slot, and the helicopter in four slot to be the second team. They dropped down to a few feet above the trees, then started toward their target. Mike and his wingman were one hundred yards behind the first two, and that perspective allowed Mike's crew to see the flash of the anti-aircraft gun when it opened up on the first element.

"Dob!" Mike called, pointing. "Do you see it?"

Dobbins, who had the gunsight on his side of the ship, nodded, then put the target in his sight. He fired the machine guns first, and Ernie saw the tracer rounds zipping in on target.

"You're on target!" Mike shouted. "Give it to 'em!"

Dobbins fired a salvo of rockets, and a few seconds later the gun pit went up in a cloud of exploding dirt, gun parts, and smoke.

"All right!" Mike shouted.

Ernie held on to the side of his seat as Mike jerked the helicopter into a violent side flare. He felt his stomach come up to his throat, and he gasped in quick, hot fear. The heavy hog shuddered under the maneuver, but the wisdom of the sudden change of flight path was immediately proven by the bright orange shower of tracer rounds that slipped through the sky where the aircraft would have been in but a second more, had Mike not taken evasive action.

By now Captain Bailey and his wingman had come around for a second pass and one of their rockets found an ammo dump. Secondary explosions erupted almost immediately and then began spreading out, following the trail of ammunition stores until soon smoke and fire covered a large portion of the area. The hootches completely disappeared, showing that they were full of ammunition.

"Son of a bitch!" Mike said. "We've got good intelligence, don't we? I thought this was supposed to be a soft LZ. Looks like another artichoke production to me."

"Whoever's making the wisecracks, knock it off," Gunslinger Six's voice said. Ernie knew that Gunslinger Six was Colonel Todaro, the owner of the private shower Mike had used. Ernie could still smell the faint perfume of the colonel's cologne, and he smiled as he thought about it.

"Gunslinger flight, stay on station until we've made the insertion," Gunslinger Six ordered.

"Roger," Bailey said. "Two, report to me when we get back."

Mike clicked the transmitter button twice. He twisted in his seat and smiled broadly at Ernie. "How'd you like it?" Mike asked.

"I was impressed," Ernie replied. He laughed nervously. "I was scared shitless, but I was impressed."

"That's what you call the old pucker factor," Mike said.

"Yes, I've heard of the puckered butthole," Ernie answered.

"There are a million stories in this hell they call a war," Mike intoned. "This is one of them." He laughed. "Think that would make a good opening paragraph?"

"I'll tell you what, Mike," Ernie replied. "If you won't try to write my story, I won't try to fly your helicopter."

"Roger on that shit," Mike replied, jerking his thumb up.

"Hey, Chief, I heard Cap'n Bailey ask you to report to him when you get back. Is he gonna get part of your ass?" Smitty asked.

"If he is, he's going to have to stand in line," Mike replied easily.

# Chapter Two

Mike killed the engine and remained in his seat filling out the dash-twelve of the logbook while the blades and gyros coasted down. Albritton unloaded the ammo chutes, then cleared and secured the guns and rocket tubes, while Smitty stood with the blade tie-down spanner in his hand, waiting for the blades to stop. Dob was carrying the vests and helmets over to a nearby Jeep. Captain Bailey walked over from his helicopter to Mike's.

"Oh-oh," Dob said. "Here comes Bailey."

Mike closed the logbook, then stepped out of the helicopter to wait for Bailey. Mike was six feet two, and heavy enough that he had to work to meet the weight requirements for the flight physical. He had dark hair and brown eyes, which he kept under glasses most of the time since his eyes were so sensitive to the sun. Captain Bailey, on the other hand, was about five feet five, so when he approached Mike he had to look up at him. Bailey saw Ernie standing on the pad by the helicopter.

"Who's this?"

"Ernie Chapel," Ernie said, sticking out his hand. "I'm with CPI. Mr. Carmack was good enough to allow me to come along with him."

"You got clearance?"

"Oh, indeed I do, Captain. I have a letter from USARV," Ernie said, pulling a letter from his shirt pocket. His shirt was wet with sweat and plastered against his skin by the flak vest he wore.

"Okay," Bailey said, waving it aside without even looking.

"What you want to see me about, Captain?" Mike asked.

Bailey turned to Mike. "Come on, Mike, you know the order about ethnic slurs," he said.

"Ethnic slurs? What ethnic slurs?"

"The artichoke thing," Bailey explained. "You know what I'm talking about. Don't think Colonel Todaro doesn't know what it refers to."

"Why, Captain, I have no idea what you are talking about," Mike said innocently.

"In a pig's ass, you don't. You're referring to the fact that Colonel Todaro is an Italian."

"Is that so? I thought he was an American."

"Of course he is," Bailey replied. "But he is of Italian ancestry."

"Now that you mention it, I believe his name does end with a vowel," Mike said.

Captain Bailey sighed and continued. "Colonel Todaro feels that as artichokes are distinctively

Italian, this constant reference to an artichoke production every time there is a screw-up is somehow a slur against him.''

"Tell me, Captain, what fruit or vegetable could we use? We couldn't use kraut, I don't suppose, or pineapple, or chili pepper, or lime. What about passion fruit? Could we use passion fruit? No, we better not, Major Alain might think we are referring to him.''

Major Alain was the Battalion S-3 officer who flew only the safest, most routine flights, yet his name came out on the air medal orders so often that many suspected he added his name to the dash-twelves when they were turned in. Major Alain was universally hated by all the pilots, and he didn't help his cause any with his irritating, almost old-maidish, effeminate personality.

Despite himself, Bailey laughed. He shook his head.

"All right, consider yourself reprimanded," he said. "On the other hand, we have two ships ready to go down to Field Maintenance. You and Rindell are up. You want to take them? You'll probably have to remain overnight in Saigon. The two replacement ships won't be ready until tomorrow morning.''

Mike looked at Bailey and smiled from ear to ear.

"Are you serious? John and I can RON in Saigon?''

"Of course, if you wanted to, I think there's a supply convoy returning late this afternoon. You could probably ride back with it if you didn't want to stay,'' Bailey said.

"No! No, we'll stay there!" Mike said. "You're not shitting me? John and I can spend the night in Saigon?"

"That's the way it works," Bailey said. "You take the ships down tonight so the crew chiefs can get all the inspection plates and panels opened before the 56th will receive them. Tomorrow morning you pick up the two they are turning out."

"Right!" Mike said. "Captain, I could kiss you."

Bailey smiled. "Careful," he said. "You might make Alain jealous."

"Say . . . uh . . . Mike," Ernie called. "If it wouldn't be too much trouble, I'd like to ride back to Saigon with you. A twenty-minute flight is a hell of a lot nicer than a two-hour drive."

"Yeah, safer, too." Mike grinned. "Every time I make that trip in a Jeep I keep a puckered asshole the whole way, just waitin' for some son of a bitch to jump out from behind the next bush with an AK-47."

"What'll we do first?" Mike asked as he, Ernie, and John met in front of the two helicopters they had just landed in front of the 56th Transportation Company hangars. The blades were still turning slowly but the crew chiefs, anxious to get their part done so they, too, would have some free time, were already pulling off doors, cowling, and inspection panels.

"What do you mean, what'll we do first?" John replied, rubbing his crotch. "Seems to me like the question here is: What'll we do second? Women! I want women!"

John was six feet tall, slimly built, blond hair

and blue eyes, with a bushy moustache. In addition to the warrant officer's bar and wings on his hat, he was also wearing a button with a picture of a glaring vulture. The vulture was saying: *Patience my ass, I want to kill.*

"Careful, John," Mike said. "I hear that a lot of the women here have some sort of rash that's contagious. Isn't that right, Ernie?"

"That's what they say," Ernie said. "Of course, I wouldn't know about that. I'm the clean-living type. What do you say I buy you guys dinner at the My Kahn?"

"Shit! You make that much money being a reporter?" Mike asked. "I mean, to just throw it around like that?"

"Not really, but I do have an expense account," Ernie said. "And you did help me get my story today. I can charge it off."

"That expense account cover a steam and cream?" John asked.

"Don't pay any attention to him, Ernie," Mike said. "He's been in the field so long that he's forgotten how to behave in polite society. On behalf of both of us, I accept your kind invitation to dine. I'll be responsible for him. You do want to eat in a nice restaurant, don't you, John, instead of a mess tent?"

"Argh! Food!" John suddenly shouted, throwing his arms in the air. "Real food! Lead me to it! Argh! Argh!"

"Jeezuz! You'll probably have to cut his meat," Ernie said.

Fifteen minutes later the three men were riding in a little blue-and-yellow Renault taxi down Cong Ly.

The driver weaved expertly in between military trucks, smoking, sputtering cyclos, bicycles, and swiftly moving Mercedes, without ever once touching the brakes. Finally he pulled to a screeching stop in front of the big white houseboat that was the My Kahn restaurant.

The restaurant was ringed with sandbags and concertina wire, and two guards stood near the gangplank, protection against the terrorist bombers who had already struck there three times.

A white-jacketed waiter escorted the three Americans to a table near the rail on the river side of the boat. The upstairs part of the restaurant was open on all sides, and cooled by a breeze that came off the river. The breeze was strong with river smells, but Ernie and the others were immune to practically all smells now, so that didn't bother them at all.

There was a bowl of salted peanuts on the table, and they began eating them as they looked at the menu. Alongside them, on the river, a boat glided by silently.

"All right," Mike said, leaning back in his chair and scratching his belly. "Look at this menu. Now this is more like it."

The menu was divided into four sections: Chinese, Vietnamese, American, and French.

"May I suggest French onion soup and coq au vin?" Ernie said.

"Sure. Why the hell not?" Mike replied, laying his menu aside. "You can order for all of us. Hey," he said. "Look at that. Look over there. Who is that?"

Mike pointed to a Vietnamese officer, dressed in

a black uniform with silver accouterments. He was carrying a black baton with a highly polished brass point, and was wearing a chrome-plated, pearl-handled pistol on his hip. He had a closely cropped moustache and flashing dark eyes, and when he laughed he displayed a shining gold tooth.

"Ah, yes," Ernie said. "That's Colonel Ngyuet Cao Mot, sometimes known as the Black Knight."

"The Black Knight?"

"His own sobriquet," Ernie said. "He does have a flare for the dramatic."

"Never mind him," John said. "Who's the woman with him? My God, that's the most beautiful woman I've ever seen."

The woman with Colonel Mot had high cheek-bones and eyes that sparkled like set jewels, framed by eyelashes as beautiful as the most delicate lace. Her skin was smooth and golden and her movements were as graceful as those of palm fronds stirred by a breeze.

"That, my friend, is Le Ngyuet Mot, the Black Knight's wife. In case you are interested, she was recently picked by *La Belle* magazine in Paris as being one of the most beautiful women in the world."

"I'll go along with that," Mike said.

Out on the river something caught Ernie's eye. He couldn't explain why it attracted his attention; it was just a boat like the other boats, but there was something about it . . . something that . . . "Jesus! Get down!" he shouted.

Not questioning the shout, Mike and John dived to the floor of the restaurant. The Black Knight and his wife were even with their table at that moment and, without thinking, Ernie dived at them, knocking them both down.

What Ernie had seen was the ugly snout of a machine gun protruding from beneath a straw mat. He had not seen it too soon, because the instant he knocked the Mots to the floor, a staccato burst of machine gun fire erupted from the river, and bullets smashed into the restaurant, shattering crystal and whistling across the floor. Women screamed and men shouted, and a waiter, carrying a heavily laden tray, fell with a thud, the front of his white jacket splashed red with his own blood.

Close on the heels of the machine gun fire, a deafening roar erupted and a searing flash of light burst from a bomb tossed aboard. Tables were shattered by the blast and in one corner the roof caved in, trapping several people under the debris.

Ernie pulled himself to an upright position and tried to look around the restaurant, but the smoke and dust hung heavily, obscuring his vision and burning his lungs with acrid fumes. His ears were still ringing from the sharpness of the explosion. He was only barely aware of the screams and cries of the injured and trapped.

Mike and John were uninjured. Ernie saw them rise slowly, brushing the dust and debris away from their uniforms.

"Son of a bitch," John said. "We don't need to come to Saigon for this kind of happy horseshit. We can get this in the field."

"You guys all right?" Ernie called.

"Yeah," Mike answered.

Out on the water the boat had veered away sharply and was making a run across the river as fast as it could be propelled by the popping little engine. Colonel Mot got to his feet and, shouting in Vietnamese to the security guards, ran to the rail. He pulled his pistol and began banging away at the little boat. The guards, who were armed with M-16s, sprayed long bursts over the rail. For a full minute the usually peaceful houseboat was turned into a full-scale battleground.

Suddenly there was a cheer from the Vietnamese on the boat.

"What the hell happened? What are they cheering about?" John asked.

Mike peered over the edge of the rail and saw two bodies floating facedown in the river while the boat, empty now, but with its engine still running, scooted toward the opposite bank.

"I think our side just scored a touchdown," Mike said sarcastically.

Everyone stood up and Ernie started to help Madam Mot to her feet. He saw that the top of her yellow *ao dai* was spattered red with blood.

"Wait," he said. "Perhaps you'd better lie there for a moment."

"I'm fine, really," Madam Mot replied. "A few little cuts from flying glass, that's all." Her voice was rich, cultured, and it caressed the English language in sensual tones.

"You!" Colonel Mot suddenly called from the rail. Ernie looked toward him, noticing the grim, almost evil expression on the colonel's face. The colonel smiled. "I want to thank you for saving our lives. What is your name?"

"Chapel, Colonel," Ernie said. "Ernie Chapel."

"An officer?" Mot looked for Ernie's insignia of rank.

"A newspaper reporter."

"A newspaper reporter? Tell me, Mr. Chapel, what will you write of this? That it was a form of patriotic expression from freedom fighters? Or that it was a terrorist attack?"

"Don't worry about Mr. Chapel, Colonel," Mike said. "He's all right."

"Indeed," Colonel Mot said. "Well, if you have the support of these young aviators, then I am convinced. I hope you can understand my concern, Mr. Chapel. I believe it is the leftist press that inflames the American protestors and prolongs this war."

Madam Mot's eyes suddenly began to flutter. Mike saw that she was about to pass out. As he grabbed her she put her arms around his neck. Her head fell back in a faint. He lowered her gently to the floor.

"Colonel, your wife!" Mike called.

Mot knelt beside her, opening the outer silk and blouse to look at her wounds. She was wearing a very delicate black lace half-bra. There were half a dozen little cuts on her smooth skin. Tiny shards of glass protruded from some of them. Colonel Mot used a set of chopsticks to pick out the glass.

"There," he said. "She'll be fine now. Again, gentlemen, you have my thanks."

# Chapter Three

Ernie leaned against the American Army ambulance and drank a cup of coffee that had been supplied by the Vietnamese Red Cross. He, Mike, and John stayed to help with the rescue work after the terrorist bomb had destroyed the My Kahn restaurant.

It was night now, and a few feet beyond the ambulance a portable generator putted noisily. A bank of floodlights sent their beams stabbing through the darkness, highlighting portions of the bombed houseboat in harsh white and stark black. The shouts of the workers drifted across the water as they climbed around the wreckage looking for more survivors.

Several hundred Vietnamese onlookers had been drawn to the scene and they stood around watching and eating pieces of fresh pineapple and dried squid. The vendors of these delicacies were enjoying a boom business as they circulated through the crowd selling their goods.

"Mr. Chapel?" a voice called, and Ernie saw one of the Vietnamese messengers from the Saigon bureau of his news agency, looking strangely out of place with his clean, crisp clothes.

"Yes?" Ernie replied, draining the rest of his coffee and stepping over to the messenger.

"The chief say you have telephone lines for one hour. You come now, please."

"What's that?" Mike asked.

Ernie sighed and hitched up his pants. "The time we can send our dispatches back is regulated by when we get the telephone lines," he said. "I've got to go. I'm sorry about the way things turned out tonight."

"Hell, don't be sorry," Mike said. He pointed to John, who was laughing with and teasing one of the Vietnamese girls working with the Red Cross. "Looks like ole John made out all right."

"What about you?"

"Hey, I'm on my own in Saigon. What can be bad about that?"

Ernie laughed. "I guess you're right," he said. "I'd like to fly with you again if you don't mind."

"Anytime, friend, anytime," Mike said.

After Ernie left, Mike waved at John to indicate that he was ready to go.

"Hey, Mike, why don't we meet at the field tomorrow?" John suggested. "I've got something going here."

"Okay," Mike agreed, and, smiling, he walked out to the street to wave over one of the noisy little cyclos that was racing by.

Mike signaled for the driver to go down rue de Pasteur, the avenue of well-kept lawns and stately villas, occupied for the most part by the high-ranking military and government officials of Vietnam. As he passed by one of the villas he noticed a Mercedes leaving the driveway. Seated in back of the car was the Black Knight. He noted the number on the fence. So, this was where Madam Mot lived.

*That's funny*, he thought. Why did he think of the house in terms of Madam Mot, instead of Colonel Mot?

When Ernie finished filing his dispatch and returned to his desk, he found Colonel Mot sitting in a chair nearby.

"Colonel Mot?"

"Ah, so you are back," Colonel Mot said. "I didn't thank you properly for saving our lives."

"No thanks necessary," Ernie said. "I was just in the right place at the right time, that's all."

"Nevertheless, I am most grateful," Mot said. "So much so that I would like to invite you to come with me. I have some entertainment planned tonight. I'm sure you will enjoy it."

"Entertainment?" Ernie asked. "What type of entertainment?"

"Oh, come, come. It's very rude to question the plans of your host. Come with me and see for yourself. I assure you, you will find it interesting."

Ernie rode in the Mercedes with Colonel Mot down Chuoung Duong Street until they came to the mass of open marketplaces primarily frequented by the Vietnamese. The merchants here were not the black marketeers of the type prevalent on Tu Do Street. Instead, they were following the customs of hundreds of years. Jabbering little Vietnamese women sifted through the markets, here buying a fish, there a head of cabbage, as they did their shopping for the evening meal.

Colonel Mot's driver stopped the car in a no-parking zone, and they walked over to the edge of the market, where they stood for a few seconds. An old woman was sitting on the sidewalk at their feet plucking fleas from the head of a little boy, who looked up at Ernie. His face was encrusted with mucus from his nose and drainage from open sores. He held his hand out, palm up, wordlessly asking for money.

Colonel Mot looked at his watch impatiently, and with that gesture, Ernie could see the wide gulf that separated Mot from his fellow countrymen who milled about him. For the average Vietnamese, there were only two times: daytime or nighttime.

"Ah, here they are," Mot said, smiling.

A two-and-one-half-ton truck braked to a stop. Two armed men jumped down from the back and looked up at the truck, their weapons ready. A man looked out of the back of the truck, terror clearly marked on his face, then disappeared back under the canvas.

A Jeep pulled up alongside the truck, mounting a .50-caliber machine gun. There was some yelling, and four men finally emerged from the back of the truck, all of them frightened and confused.

"One of these young men threw the bomb at the My Kahn," Mot said.

"I thought the bomb came from the boat and both of those people were killed."

"The boat was just a diversion," Mot explained. "The bomb was thrown from the street."

"Which one of these men did it?"

"I'm not sure," Colonel Mot said. "But they know which of them is guilty, and that makes them all equally guilty."

"I don't understand," Ernie said. "Why are they here?"

"Perhaps a public execution will discourage others from the same foolishness," Mot suggested.

"You're going to execute them right here, in the public square?"

"Yes," Mot said. "And you are going to write about it."

"Colonel Mot, the Saigon government will never win the support of the people in this way," Ernie said.

Mot laughed a short, cryptic laugh. "We don't need their support, Mr. Chapel," he said, taking in the people of the market with a wave of his hand. "All we need is their fear. And for that, there is nothing better than a public execution."

The guards moved the four men into position against the wall of one of the nearby buildings. The bolt on the Jeep-mounted machine gun was slammed home.

"My God, Mot!" Ernie gasped. "You're not going to execute them with a .50-caliber machine gun? Those rounds are as big as a man's fist! They'll chop them up like ground meat."

"But their deaths will be sure," Mot said.

Dirty children, their skin covered with scabs and their hair full of lice, edged closer to the Jeep. They put their fingers in their ears and waited patiently to move in and strip the bodies as soon as the firing stopped.

While Ernie watched in disbelief and horror, the gun opened up, not popping like a small gun, but exploding in earthshaking, stomach-jarring blasts.

The little men began to fly apart. Arms and legs were literally shredded. One of them was completely cut in half. The top of his body toppled over backward, and the bottom half stood for a moment gushing blood, then fell forward.

Suddenly the gun stopped, and the relative silence of the bickering Vietnamese again filled the air. Only the children watched; the vendors and the buyers seemed oblivious to the killings.

Ernie stood there for several seconds fighting the nausea. Mot pulled a silk handkerchief from his pocket and wiped his hands vigorously. His eyes had a demonic glow.

"I thought that since you were directly involved with the bombing, you would be pleased to see that justice was done," he said.

Ernie couldn't speak. He was unable to force the words through the grim sense of shock he felt.

"Well," Mot said, seeing how Ernie was reacting, "perhaps I misjudged your threshold of sensitivity. We'll go now. I have arranged something that I'm sure you will enjoy."

Ernie followed Mot, but it was almost by reflex. He was anxious to get away from the scene of horror, where the children were now fighting with one another for possession of the clothes the prisoners had been wearing. He looked away as the car drove off, and he breathed deeply to fight the nausea.

"I'm sorry you weren't entertained," Mot said, as if apologizing for recommending a bad movie to a friend. "I suppose I tend to forget that not everyone shares my lust for blood. There is something very exciting about the sudden death of an enemy."

"You aren't saying that just to shock me, are you?" Ernie asked. "You really mean it."

"Yes, yes, of course I mean it." Mot laughed. "It even gets me sexually excited. Explain that to me, if you can."

"I'm afraid I can't." Ernie replied.

A few minutes later, Mot's driver stopped the car in front of a building in Cholon. There was a large wall around the building and a private guard stood by the gate.

"What is this place?" Ernie asked.

"I promised you some entertainment, and now I'm going to deliver. You didn't like the other, but I know you'll like this," Mot replied. "Come, we'll go inside."

The grounds inside the wall were laid out in a beautiful garden with box hedges, tiny, beautifully trimmed trees, and a red-and-gold bridge arching gracefully over a quiet pool. An old woman handed them each a dressing gown and a towel, and directed them toward a room where they were met by two beautiful women who indicated that they were there to bathe them.

"I thought you might enjoy this," Mot said as

he settled down into his bathtub. There was a bamboo screen separating his bathtub from the one used by Ernie, so that they couldn't see each other, but they could talk.

"This is more to my liking," Ernie agreed. The bath was sensual and relaxing. The girl assigned to him was beautiful. She was wearing only panties and a brassiere, but Ernie intuitively knew that she was not a prostitute . . . and he was glad.

After the bath Ernie wrapped himself in a large towel and went into a small room that opened just off the big bathroom. There was a bed in the room, and a small electric fan played a cool breeze across the bed.

Ernie put on the comfortable dressing gown and then lay down on the bed. He closed his eyes to luxuriate in the total comfort, and had almost gone to sleep when he was roused by a gentle voice.

"Colonel Mot has sent me to you. I hope I am worthy."

Ernie opened his eyes in surprise and looked at the girl standing by his bed. She was totally nude, and her skin was beautiful and without blemish. She was nearly without curves as well, having only tiny suggestions of breasts. The girl couldn't have been more than twelve years old.

"What?" Ernie asked.

"I am here to make love to you," the girl said with a shy smile. "I hope you find me pleasing."

"No!" Ernie protested.

Tears sprang to the young girl's eyes. "You find me ugly?"

"Em," Ernie said, using the Vietnamese term of

affection, "Colonel Mot has played a trick on you. I think you are very pretty . . . but I cannot do it."

"It won't work?" the girl asked, pointing toward Ernie's groin, her face registering sympathy for him.

"That's right," Ernie said, deciding it was easier to let the girl believe that. "It's not your fault. Colonel Mot doesn't have to find out."

Across Cholon, on the other side of Saigon, Mike lay on a sleeping mat in a small room behind a twisting alley off Truh Minh Gang. Beside him lay the girl he had brought from Maxim's Bar. On a mat on the far side of the room slept the girl's eighteen-month-old baby. The angry snarl of a helicopter sounded overhead as a Huey returned from the night courier flight to Vung Tau. With no thought at all, Mike could transport himself into the cockpit with the red, winking instrument panel, the JP-4 scented breeze through the window, the feel of power in his hands and feet as the ship answered his command. For a moment he was one with the crew. He smiled as he wondered what they would think if they knew that one of them was below, with a woman, in the dark cluster of buildings, shacks, and lean-tos that was Saigon.

"You must stay till morning, now," the girl said. "If you go on street now, you get picked up by MP's."

"I'll stay," Mike said.

The girl shifted her body closer to him. "That be five hundred more P," she said.

Outside, Mike could hear the clack of the soup

vendor's sticks as he made his final rounds of the night. The city was going to sleep. He wondered if Madam Mot was in bed.

# Chapter Four

Ernie could feel the C-130s before he could hear them, and he could hear them before he could see them. It started as a rumble, deep in the pit of his stomach, then a roar in his ears. Finally the ghostly shapes sliding through the early morning mist materialized as giant four-engined transport aircraft, touching down on the landing mat of perforated steel planking with a growl of authority.

Ernie had flown into staging area Swift Strike with Mike, and now he sat on the damp ground under a tree, sucking on the sweet tip of a blade of grass. They had come in the dark of pre-dawn, and Ernie sat with Mike, John, and the others, watching the morning mist roll in to mask the break of day.

All along the outer dike stood a long line of

hogs, bristling with guns and rocket tubes. Alongside their ships, sprawled out on the grass in various stages of rest, were the other pilots in Mike's company.

"Hurry up and wait, hurry up and wait," John grumbled. "Damn, I get tired of this shit."

"So did the men who served in Caesar's legions," Ernie said.

"Yeah, you old fart, and you were probably there to write about it, weren't you?" Mike teased.

"My earliest campaign was the Peloponnesian War," Ernie replied.

"You did write about World War Two, didn't you?"

"Yeah," Ernie said.

"That was the real one," John observed.

Ernie thought of the hell of Iwo Jima. "They're all real," he said.

"There're the guys we're taking in," Mike said, pointing to the Vietnamese soldiers who were off-loading from the C-130s. "Son of a bitch! Look at that. Ernie, isn't that the Black Knight?"

Ernie saw Colonel Mot standing by the tail ramp of one of the transports, watching his men as they filed off.

"That's him, all right."

"Look, all those guys are dressed in black," John observed. "How the hell are we supposed to know them from the V.C.?"

"I don't know," Mike said. "I guess if anyone shoots at us, we'll just shoot back."

"Colonel Mot has just received permission for his special-attack elements to wear black," Ernie explained. "It's psychological."

"Psychological," John said. "Now, ain't that the shits?"

Ernie couldn't help but be impressed with the array of equipment the Black Knight was bringing in for the mission. There were hundreds of troops in full battle gear, helicopters stretching from one end of the field to the other, and a steady train of C-130s coming in at three-minute intervals.

A door gunner walked by, wearing a flak vest with a gunship painted on the back. The ship had eyes and teeth and was carrying a bloody sword in one of the landing skids that had been drawn like a hand. Beneath the drawing was the door gunner's credo in blood-red letters: *I fly for the only truly nonprejudiced genocide unit in the world. I will kill anyone, anywhere, anytime, regardless of race, creed, color, age, or sex. No questions asked, no quarter given.*

"Now, that's one mean son of a bitch," John chuckled, pointing to the door gunner.

Ernie laughed, then looked over at the two warrant officers who were the pilot and co-pilot for the door gunner's ship. They were sitting on a log and one of them pulled out a plug of chewing tobacco, sliced off a long, thin piece, then handed the plug to the other. The other also cut off a piece. Then, in unison, they stuck the tobacco in their mouths, which were barely discernible beneath the heavy moustaches each of them wore. They chewed silently, unaware that they were the subject of Ernie's observation.

Ernie felt he had seen this same scene before, like déjà vu. Then he knew where he had seen them. The steely eyes, the rakish moustaches, the youthful bravado — all had been duplicated in hundreds of Matthew Brady pictures from the Civil War.

Colonel Mot came walking by, laughing and talking with Colonel Todaro. As usual, Colonel Mot was followed by an entourage of Ernie's contemporaries. Ernie had little respect for them; they were the newsmen who always went for the easy story. They would get a few pictures and quotes from Mot, then file their pieces and beat it back to the eighth-floor bar of the Hotel Caravel in downtown Saigon. In the meantime, Ernie and a few of the harder-working reporters would be slogging through the jungle.

"Follow close behind me, gentlemen," Colonel Mot told those who were with him, "and you will never miss the action. I go to the sound of the guns and bathe in the wash of battle."

"Colonel Mot, there's been some talk in high levels about your political ambitions. Is there any foundation to this talk?" one of the reporters asked.

"I am not actively seeking any political recognition," Colonel Mot answered. "In fact, quite the opposite is true. Any position less than that of President would cause me to fail in my duty to give my country my utmost."

"Then you are interested in the President's job?"

"You are presuming a great deal," Colonel Mot replied with a small smile. "But, to answer your question, I would gladly serve in that capacity if I thought it would be best for the nation." Colonel Mot looked over at Ernie and the air crews and smiled. "Gentlemen, let me introduce you to a real warrior's reporter. Notice how Mr. Chapel stays away from headquarters to be with the fighting men."

"Yes," Don Wright of CBS-TV answered. "We've met." Ernie and Wright had had a couple of run-ins before. Wright had the idea that the power of his medium should give him special privileges, and he had tried to capitalize on that more than once. Some of the other reporters let him get away with it . . . Ernie wouldn't.

Mot walked on and the entourage followed him as the cameramen moved to get into position for the best shot.

"Holy shit!" Mike said. "You'd think he was winning the war by himself."

"He's what they call good copy," Ernie said.

"Mike," someone called. "The briefing tent is set up. They're calling for all the pilots now."

"Do you mind if I go to the briefing with you?" Ernie asked.

Mike chuckled. "Why do you want to? I'm not what they call good copy, am I?"

"You'll do until something better comes along," Ernie said.

Ernie followed Mike, John, Dobbins, and all the other pilots of the gunship company to the tent. There they saw the pilots of the airlift companies, as well as the dustoff and helicopter recovery pilots. The Vietnamese infantry officers also joined them and the briefing began.

The first part of the briefing was for the aviators. They received weather, intelligence, med-evac, and helicopter recovery procedures. Then Colonel Mot, speaking in English and in Vietnamese, told the purpose of the mission. The V.C., he said, had gathered a strong force at Binh Loi, and he intended to crush that force.

The mist had burned away by the time the briefing got under way, and Ernie was surprised to see that the briefing tent had actually been pitched on the edge of the lawn of a large French villa. Two blond-haired children ran laughing through a jungle-gym set, the sound of their laughter floating in occasionally to contrast sharply with the continual drone of aircraft engines as the C-130s began leaving. The children played as if they were totally alone, completely oblivious of the strike force that was gathered nearby.

After the briefing, Ernie walked back to the gunship parking area. He stood beside the open door with the sun beating down on his back, looking inside at the jump seat that had been rigged for him. During the actual mission everyone on board the helicopter would have a job to do. The pilot would fly the ship, the co-pilot would fire the mounted guns, the door gunner and crew chief would fire the door guns, but Ernie would just sit there. It was a terrifying experience, made more so by his feeling of helplessness.

"What'd the bigwigs say in there, Mr. Chapel?" SP-5 Smith asked. He was checking the ammunition in the chutes that ran from the boxes inside. "We about ready to spool up?"

"Spool up?" Ernie replied, not understanding the question.

"Yeah, you know, start engines," Smitty explained, making a circular motion with his finger.

"The turbine engines spin like a spool; that's where we get the word."

"Oh, yes," Ernie said. "I think we're about ready."

"Why don't you climb in on your seat now?" Smitty invited. "That way me 'n Albritton can mount our guns and string our monkey straps."

Ernie climbed into the helicopter and settled in the red nylon seat that was mounted in the center, just behind the console, facing forward. He saw the crews of the other helicopters getting aboard. Then Mike and Mr. Dobbins got in. John Rindell was flying the ship just behind them.

In the distance, toward the briefing area, a green flare arced through the sky. That was the signal to start engines. Mike pulled the starter trigger. Within seconds the T53-L11 turbine engine, which was nestled in the cowling behind them, was a roaring inferno of white-hot flames, spinning a turbine thousands of revolutions per minute and transmitting that power to the rotor blades overhead. As the auxiliary systems kicked in, the warning lights winked out and the chopper sat poised, ready to leap into the air.

"This is Swift Strike control," Ernie heard a voice say. "Gunslinger, you are cleared for immediate departure."

"Up," Mike said, and he pulled the collective control stick up, lifting the helicopter off the ground. He made a slight pedal correction for torque, then departed over the large French villa with the kids still playing unconcernedly below them.

Ernie twisted around in his seat and stared out through the open door, over the barrel of Smitty's M-60, at the ground below.

"Red team left, Blue team right," a voice said, and Mike moved the helicopter to the left to become part of Red team, flying cover for the UH-1D lift helicopters that would be carrying the troops.

The UH-1Ds were lifting off then, moving into a flight formation of V's. Ernie watched two of them as they climbed up alongside . . . Then he witnessed a moment of horror. Two of the Hueys, loaded with fourteen human beings each, meshed their rotor blades. Because of the sound of the engines Ernie heard nothing . . . it was as if the terrible drama was being played on silent film. One moment both helicopters were flying along smoothly in graceful formation; the next moment they were throwing rotor blades and other pieces of debris as they began tumbling, sickeningly, to earth, eight hundred feet below.

"My God!" someone shouted. "Their rotors meshed!"

Ernie watched both helicopters tumble all the way to the ground, then explode in two rosettes of fire.

"Gunslinger Six, is the mission aborted?" someone called.

"Negative," Gunslinger Six replied. "Dustoff, check for survivors."

"Roger," Dustoff answered.

"Where were they from?" Mike asked over the intercom.

"Sixty-eighth, I think," Dobbins answered. "Top Tiger."

There was no more conversation about the two helicopters or anything else that didn't relate strictly to business. The lift element proceeded to Binh Loi. Then the gunships, Mike's included, made a few passes at the treeline around the landing zone. Ernie watched as their tracer rounds and rockets zipped into the treelines, though he didn't notice any return fire.

"This is Red team leader. Anybody pick up any return fire?"

"This is Red Four. I think I did, off to the left."

"Near the rocks?"

"That's affirm."

"Uh . . . okay, Red team, make one more pass concentrating on the rocks. Then stand by for the insertion."

Mike brought the gunship back around, standing it on the rotor as he made the turn. The area around the rocks was burning now, but try as he could, Ernie still didn't see anything.

"There ain't shit down there," Mike said disgustedly as they pulled away from their last pass.

The gunships flew back and forth along the edge of the open rice paddy that was being used as the landing zone while the UH-1Ds touched down, off-loaded their troops, then took off again. When the last lift helicopter was empty and the infantrymen were clear of the LZ, the helicopters were ordered back to the staging area. There was nothing to do now except stay on standby to be called out immediately if needed.

Once back in the staging area the ships were refueled and reloaded while the crews moved over to rest in the shade of the trees and enjoy the soft breeze.

"Follow me to the sound of the guns, my ass," Mike laughed, recalling Colonel Mot's comment earlier in the morning. "If I ever saw a candy-ass LZ, this was it."

"Didn't bother me any," Dobbins said, folding his hands behind his head. "This is the kind I like."

Suddenly their conversation was interrupted by rifle fire. The shots cracked out sharply and echoed through the trees so that no one could tell where they were coming from. Word was passed down that a Viet Cong patrol had been contacted and that everyone in the staging area was to stay behind cover.

"Shit!" Mike said, pulling his pistol as he inched up to the top of the berm and looked out into the foliage. "Now we know why the LZ was soft! The sons of bitches are here!"

The firing continued sharply for several moments more. Ernie, who wasn't armed, peered intently into the darkened interior of the copse. He felt a knot of fear in his stomach as the bullets whistled by, snapping into the tree trunks and popping through the leaves. Then the firing ceased abruptly.

There was silence for a moment, then some shouts, and Ernie saw a dustoff crew running for their helicopter. By the time they had it started there were some people running from the trees, carrying wounded on a stretcher. One of the wounded was an American G.I., and the other was a V.C. At least Ernie thought he was V.C., but he heard someone say he was friendly.

"They're ARVN. They're wearing black, and when they came back from their patrol some new guys took 'em for V.C. and opened up. They's two of 'em dead back there," a young soldier explained.

The Dustoff ship took off over them then with a whine of its engine and pop of its blades.

"Did you say this was a soft LZ, Mike?" Ernie asked. "With the twenty-eight killed in the helicopter collision and these two, this one cost thirty lives."

"Yeah," Mike said. "Guess it wasn't all that soft after all."

# Chapter Five

Ernie walked over to the cooler and punched the button to draw out a cup of water. A large bubble formed in the inverted glass tank, then popped up to the surface with a gurgle. He stood at the window as he sipped the cool water and looked out at the traffic on Nguyen Hue street. The street was crowded with smoking cyclos, blue-and-yellow taxicabs, and military Jeeps and trucks of all sizes and services. Hundreds of Vietnamese men scurried about in uniform, many in the distinctive Tiger uniforms, though Ernie knew that few of them had ever actually been in the field.

Behind him a dozen typewriters clacked and dinged as CPI correspondents worked on their stories. One of them, Jerry Decker, looked up.

"Hey, Ernie, what's that chopper pilot's name?

You know, the gunship jock you been ridin' with? Carmack, isn't it?''

"Yeah," Ernie said, turning around. "Why? Has anything happened to him?"

"Not that I know of," Jerry answered. "But this came through from USARV PIO. Thought you might be interested."

Jerry held out a sheet of paper and Ernie took it from him. It was an extract from an awards orders.

## HEADQUARTERS

## USARV

## APO U.S. Forces 96307

SPECIAL ORDER NUMBER 291    11 Sept 1968

## EXTRACT

14. DA 348. By direction of the Secretary of the Army, following individual is authorized to accept the award of the VIETNAMESE CROSS OF GALLANTRY.

CARMACK, MICHAEL TIMOTHY, W2214390 CW3 671B HQ USARV APO 96307

ADMINISTRATIVE DATA

Auth: Para 3-58, Sec XV LTR 14 Jun 1963
HOR: Sikeston, Missouri
PLEAD: Fort Rucker, Alabama

SPECIAL INSTRUCTIONS

Award will be presented by Colonel Ngyuet Cao
Mot, CO Special (Strike) Forces, ARVN

FOR THE COMMANDER

T.J. Hunsinger
Colonel, GS
Chief of Staff


OFFICIAL:

ROBERT A. BIVENS
1LT, AGC
Asst Adj gen

DISTRIBUTION: 110 AG Gen Mail Gra, 5 AG
Orders, 10 Individual indic, 2 CG USARV, 2
HQDA
(DAAG-ASO-O) Wash DC 20315, 2 HQDA
(DA-PO-OPD-WOAVN) Wash DC 20315
C-I-T-A-T-I-O-N

In that Chief Warrant Officer-3 Michael T. Carmack, W2214390, did distinguish himself by
heroism while participating in aerial flight as
evidenced by voluntary action above and beyond
the call of duty, to wit: CW-3 Carmack, on the
morning of 11 July, 1968, while flying support for an
infantry insertion, did, with great disregard for his
own safety, proceed against anti-aircraft
emplacements eliminating the position and allowing the insertion of troops to continue. CW-3 Car-

mack's dedication to duty in the face of extreme danger did ensure the success of the mission. Mr. Carmack's actions were in keeping with the highest traditions of the military service, and of the cooperative counter-insurgent operations of the combined powers of the United States and the Republic of Vietnam, and reflect great credit to himself and the United States Army.

For the Commander

WILLIAM C. WESTMORELAND
Commanding General
United States Forces, Vietnam

OFFICIAL:

ROBERT A. BIVENS
1LT, AGC
Asst Adg Gen

"Well, I'll be damned," Ernie said. "When is the award to be given?"

"Two o'clock this afternoon. USARV has laid on a chopper for any reporters who want to go. You want me to reserve you a seat?"

"Yeah," Ernie said. "I think I'll go up and watch."

"Okay," Jerry said, picking up the phone. "I'll call and hold you a seat. Seems to me like it's pretty tame stuff, though."

Ernie didn't tell Jerry that he'd been along on the same mission. He wanted to go because he felt a proprietary interest in the ceremony.

There were a half a dozen reporters on the chopper going up. Two of them were TV reporters who also had their cameramen along. Ernie and the other print reporters had only their canvas bags with cameras, tablets, and pencils.

As the chopper approached Phu Loi, it banked over the 605th DS shed. A familiar sign was painted on the roof:

SEE SEVEN STATES FROM ROCK CITY
ATOP LOOKOUT MOUNTAIN

The blades popped loudly as the helicopter settled through the air it was spilling. The pilot stopped the descent a few feet above the ground, then hovered over to a pad and set it down. The reporters were out before the blades quit spinning.

Ernie hurried over to Mike's tent, where he found his friend dressed in khakis. Ernie stuck out his hand in congratulations.

"If you ask me, I'm a little embarrassed by it," Mike said. "I wasn't the only pilot that day. Hell, I wasn't even in charge of the flight."

"Maybe not, but your helicopter is the one that destroyed the anti-aircraft guns."

"Then what about the other guys in my ship?" Mike asked. "My co-pilot, gunner, crew chief . . . hell, even you. You were on board that day."

"I just went along for the ride," Ernie said.

"Nevertheless, I don't know why the hell I've been singled out," Mike said. "And if they are going to give it to me, why don't they just slip it through distribution? Why make such a big fuss about it?"

"Maybe the Black Knight likes you," Ernie suggested.

"Hey," John said. "Maybe the Black Knight's wife likes you."

"I'm sure that's it," Mike answered quickly. His answer was a little sharper than he intended because, for some strange reason, he had been unable to get Madam Mot out of his mind from the first moment he saw her.

Back in Saigon, Le stepped out of the bathtub and wrapped herself in a purple towel. A faint aromatic trace of specially blended perfume followed her as she walked from the bathroom to her dressing room and stood there, trying to decide what she would wear to the award ceremony. She had surprised her husband when she told him she wanted to go.

She wanted to go because she wanted to see the American pilot again. From the moment she saw him in the My Kahn, she had woven sexual fantasies around him.

Le dropped her towel and reached for her dress. For a moment she was totally nude and a breath of air caressed her naked skin. She shivered and thought of the American pilot.

Le decided to occupy her mind with haiku, poems of exactly seventeen syllables. When perfectly constructed, they were like pebbles cast into the pool of the mind, sending out ripples of association.

Is that a dancing angel . . . on the tree . . . ? It is a beam of sunlight.

It was necessary that she engage in such mental

exercise or her mind would run away with thoughts of sex. Sex with Mike Carmack. She could imagine herself in bed with him, feeling him inside her.

The lovers come together . . . mouth to mouth . . . leg to leg . . . fountain flowing.

Le no longer tried to push the thoughts aside. She allowed Mike to make love to her in her mind. She drifted sensually with her erotic thoughts, losing herself in sexual fantasy.

As the band played, the echo of the drum and bass horn floated back from the walls of the hangar buildings, arriving about one half-beat after the melody so that the music came out in a strange, cacophonous sound in march time. The warrant officer who was directing the band was aware of the off-beat echo, and he both quickened and slowed the chop of his baton to try to regulate it, though without success.

Mike stood all alone in the middle of the field, sweating profusely under the hot sun, cursing under his breath, annoyed that he was not only having to go through all this, but that he was having to subject his men to it as well. It was especially galling to him that he was singled out when his performance was no more heroic than anyone else's.

Colonel Mot stopped in front of Mike. Mot was wearing a black satin flying suit, a red neck scarf, and exceptionally dark sunglasses. The sunglasses were American Army flight glasses. His wife, standing behind him, was wearing them as well.

Mot looked over at Colonel Todaro, who cleared his throat and stepped up to a microphone.

"Attention to orders," Todaro read. "Headquarters, United States Army, Vietnam, Special Orders two ninety-one. Chief Warrant Officer Three Michael Timothy Carmack is hereby awarded the Vietnamese Cross of Gallantry for performance above and beyond the call of duty.''

Todaro went on to read the citation, droning through it in such a monotone that if Mike ever thought he deserved the award, he would have changed his mind after the reading. Finally Todaro finished and stepped away from the microphone, then looked at the Black Knight and nodded.

"So, Mr. Carmack, we meet again," Mot said quietly. "I hope you don't mind if I allow my wife the honor of pinning on your medal. You made quite an impression on her during your brief meeting in the My Kahn.''

Mot stepped aside and held out a box toward his wife. She drew the gold pendant with its red-and-yellow ribbon from the felt lining.

"From a grateful people, Mr. Carmack," Le said in a soft, silken voice.

"Thank you, Madam Mot," Mike said.

"Mr. Carmack, I'm sponsoring a small reception in my home this afternoon, in your honor. Your commanding officer told me you would be happy to attend."

"You might say it's a command performance, Mr. Carmack," Mot added. "You will be there, of course?''

"Of course, sir," Mike answered.

"At two," Le said. She slipped her glasses off and looked directly at Mike. There was something about the expression in her face, the look in her eyes, which disturbed him, and he felt himself flush under her intense gaze.

"And now, my dear, we must go," Colonel Mot said. "We have a few calls to make before the reception."

Mike stood at attention as Colonel Mot and Le left the field. The battalion adjutant dismissed the formation. Mike walked toward his tent.

The Vietnamese Cross of Gallantry was really a medal of little significance, and many men had already received the award at least once. Generally they were handed out without ceremony. The ceremony was what made this one so unusual, and Mike's fellow pilots knew he was embarrassed by it. Therefore, they offered profuse congratulations as a form of good-natured teasing.

"Listen," John said, putting his finger under the medal and pulling it out from Mike's shirt, holding it so that it caught the sunlight and flashed brilliantly. "Where do you think we could get this hero something to drink?"

"The officers' club?"

"No, let's not share him with the masses yet. How 'bout the pilots' lounge?"

Under their prodding, Mike agreed to go to the pilots' lounge to "celebrate" the award. As they started across the perforated steel planking, he felt someone looking at him. Then he saw that Madam Mot was standing by her husband's car, staring at him from behind her dark glasses.

"Yeah, the lounge," he said, anxious to get away. "That sounds good. Let's go have a beer."

"Come along, Ernie," John invited. "We'll put

all the marks by Mike's name." That was a reference to the fact that a drink tally sheet was kept posted on the refrigerator door, and every time someone got a beer they put a mark by their name, then settled at the end of the month.

"So, how does it feel to be a hero?" John asked as he stabbed holes in the tops of the cans of beer and passed them around. Beer spewed out each time he punched the opener in, and foam bubbled invitingly over the top of the cans.

Mike took a long drink from his can before he answered. "It feels phony," he said.

"Yeah, well, it gave the troops a chance to stand in the noonday sun," John said. He looked at Dobbins and laughed. "And it saved Dob a little money. He was going to head on down to Plantation Road and buy a little Saigon tea for the whores."

"Well, bless their little hearts," Dob said. "They're such friendly little girls, and they're always thirsty."

"Now, there's someone I wouldn't mind buying a little Saigon tea for," one of the officers said, pointing with his beer can toward Madam Mot.

"You and me both," John said. "I'll tell you, she is the most beautiful damned dink I've ever seen."

"Hell, you can go down to Maxim's on Plantation Road and find at least five as pretty as she is," Dob said. "Big Boobs, for example, or the Rabbit Girl, or Brandy, or even Ammo Bearer."

John laughed. "Dob has this area laid out,

doesn't he? Think he doesn't know where to get a steam and cream?''

"Ah, that's just my little corner of the world here at Phu Loi," Dob said. He looked at Ernie, who had been quiet for the whole time. "Now Mr. Chapel, there, is the one to talk to. He's a high-paid, famous journalist. A civilian who can go anywhere he wants, anytime he wants. If there's a corner on the poontang market in Vietnam, it's people like Ernie Chapel who have it sewed up. Right, Ernie?''

"Wish I could say yes," Ernie said. He pointed across the way toward one of the television reporters who had come up with him. The reporter was squatting in the middle of a road, holding one hand on top of his helmet as if to keep it on, while with the other he held a microphone in front of his mouth. Behind him a half-dozen South Vietnamese soldiers were running toward a treeline, shooting, then diving to the ground as if they were under fire. The cameraman was taking it all in. "There's the glory-and-glamour guys . . . the TV reporters.''

"You think someone will be watching that shit in their living rooms tomorrow night, believing they're seeing real action?" one of the officers asked.

"Does a fat dog fart?" John asked. He crushed his beer can and tossed it into an empty fifty-five-gallon drum. "That makes my ass knit barbed wire. Why don't you write about that sometime, Ernie? About the TV reporters who manufacture stories?''

"I can't," Ernie said.

"You can't? Why not?"

"It would seem self-serving. You know, the TV guys are phony, we're the only ones real, so turn off TV and read your newspapers. No one would believe me."

"Yeah, well, when I get back I'm going to tell 'em," John said.

"What makes you think anyone will listen?" Dob asked.

# Chapter Six

That afternoon Mike parked his Jeep in the court-
yard of the Mot villa. From inside the walls of the
estate it was impossible to tell that this elegant
home was situated in Vietnam, surrounded on all
four sides by contrasting filth and squalor. Here,
fountains splashed and flowers blossomed, and
trees shaded a baroque-style Mediterranean house
that wouldn't have been out of place on the
Riviera.

A servant met Mike and escorted him into the
house. The inside of the house was a mixture of
French and Oriental decor, but whereas these two
schools blended in cooking, they did not blend well
in decorating. The house was a horrid mishmash of
ostentatiousness. Huge, deep blue Ming vases com-

peted for space with Monet originals and Louis XIV furniture.

"Ah, Mr. Carmack, how good of you to come," Mot said. "My wife will be pleased."

Mot was wearing a white sharkskin suit with a lime-green shirt. It was the first time Mike had ever seen him out of uniform. He was standing at the bar, pouring himself a drink. He held the bottle of Canadian Mist up for Mike, and Mike nodded yes.

"Where is your wife?" Mike asked. "And where are the others?"

"The others?" Mot asked innocently. "What others?"

"For the reception," Mike said. "You did say there was to be a reception here this afternoon?"

"Yes," Mot said. He tasted his drink and smacked his lips appreciatively. "But there are no others, dear boy. There is just you."

"Just me?"

"Are you disappointed?" Madam Mot inquired. Her voice was smooth and throaty.

Mike looked toward the sound of her voice and gasped. She was wearing the traditional *ao dai*, but the silk pants that were normally worn beneath the long, free-flowing outer garment were absent. The *ao dai* was split from her waist to her feet on each side, and beneath the *ao dai* there was nothing except a long, lovely expanse of naked leg and thigh.

"Do you like my wife's mode of dress?" Colonel Mot asked, laughing. "She has singlehandedly changed one thousand years of dressing custom by discarding the long silk pants. You must admit, it does do much for the costume."

"Your wife is a lovely woman," Mike said truthfully.

"Yes, well, I'm sure the two of you will have a wonderful time this afternoon," Mot said. He put his empty glass down on the bar. "I must be going."

"Going? Colonel Mot, you mean you aren't going to stay here?"

"No," Mot said lightly. "It's my wife's reception, not mine."

Mike watched, dumbfounded, as Mot left. Then he turned back toward Madam Mot. "I don't understand what's going on here," he said.

"Surely, Mr. Carmack, you have some idea. After all, you are a big boy," Madam Mot said. She reached behind her to release the catch of her bra. Then she removed it, pulling it from under the *ao dai* so that the nipples of her breasts stood in bold relief against the silk of the garment. "If you think about it, you'll understand," she said. "Think of hot blood, the mingling of flesh, yours hard and driving, mine soft and yielding."

"Madam Mot . . ."

"Call me Le," Le said. She moved closer to him and Mike was aware of a soft fragrance, tantalizing, but not overpowering. "Let's have a drink, shall we?"

Le poured a smoky liquid into two small glasses and handed one to Mike. They touched glasses briefly. Then Mike drank the liquor, feeling it burn throughout his whole body and bringing heat to his loins.

An old lady padded into the room, moving

quietly on bare feet. Her sudden and unexpected appearance startled Mike. The old woman spoke in singsong Vietnamese.

"What is it?" Mike asked.

Le smiled. "Haung has prepared our bath."

"Our bath?"

"Yes," Le said. She put her hand on Mike's arm and led him from the room, down a hall, and into a bathroom, then pointed inside. Steam was rising from an enormous sunken tub, and the scent of bath perfume filled the air.

"I've never seen a bathtub so large," Mike said. "It looks like it was built for two people."

Le smiled. "It was." She picked up a purple robe and handed it to Mike. "Here," she said, pointing to the bedroom. "Remove your clothes and put on this robe. Don't enter the bathroom until you hear me call."

By now any anxiety Mike may have felt was gone, replaced by a strong, growing, sexual desire. Eagerly, he went into the bedroom and took off his uniform to put on the robe. He already had an erection, and as he moved, the contact with the robe sent tiny electric shocks coursing through him.

"You may come in, Mr. Carmack," Le called.

Mike opened the door and saw Le standing beside the tub. The robe she wore was also purple and delightfully short, revealing long, shapely golden legs.

"I want to be your tender teacher, Mike," Le said in her low, throaty voice. "One of the things I want to teach you is the sexually invigorating properties of the bath. Now, if you would be so kind as to turn your back, I shall step into the water.''

''Why can't I watch?'' Mike asked.

''Patience, dear boy,'' Le said, smiling at him. ''Please have patience.''

Obeying her, Mike turned his back. He heard the soft rippling of water as she settled into the bath.

''Now, if you would step in, please?''

Mike allowed the robe to drop to the floor, then started to turn around.

''No, don't turn yet,'' she said.

Still facing away from her, he stepped into the water, then sat down.

''Now you may turn.''

When Mike turned toward her he could see the golden gleam of her breasts, adorned but not concealed by the bath suds. One of her nipples peeked through the bubbles and it was maddening to his senses. He reached for her.

''No,'' she said sharply. Then, more softly: ''Please, Mike, don't be impatient. You will enjoy it so much more, believe me.''

''All right,'' Mike said. ''Whatever you say.''

''That's a good boy.'' Le smiled, and she raised a washcloth to her breast and squeezed water so that some of the suds were washed away.

As they bathed, Mike noticed that he was gradually able to see more and more of her body. At first he thought it was an accidental exposure. Then he realized that it was a studied movement as she wiped away more of the suds. Each minute after tantalizing minute, she opened more of herself to his view until every delightful curve was finally laid bare. But only briefly, because as soon as she had removed the last of the suds and was completely exposed, she stepped out of the tub and covered herself with a large towel. For one maddening instant, she had been totally nude. And then, once again, her body was protected from his gaze. She walked into the bedroom and he, wrapping himself in an oversized towel, followed.

"Would you?" she asked, holding up a flask of oil. The oil was an amber color, and the glow shining through it made it appear as if it had an inner fire.

"Yes," Mike said. His tongue was thick and his throat dry and he found it extremely difficult to talk. He took the flask, half expecting it to be hot from its brilliance. Le turned her back to him, then removed her robe.

Mike took a short breath of appreciation at the sight of her nudity. The smooth flow of her skin continued in an unbroken line from her shoulders down her gently curved back, across the soft mounds of her buttocks, split by the smooth fold between the cheeks, and on down her thighs and calves, ending in perfectly proportioned ankles and feet.

Le stretched out on her stomach, and Mike poured some of the oil on her beautiful golden skin, then began rubbing. The sensuousness of it moved through his fingers and inflamed his whole body until he was consumed by desire.

"Now, my beautiful American flyer," Le said in a voice that was low with her own passion. She turned over and held her arms up in invitation to him, beckoning him down to her. "Make love to me now."

Mike moved over her and Le put her arms around his neck and pulled him to her, taking his tongue deep into her mouth, then pushing it back with her own tongue thrusting into his mouth. Mike abandoned himself, subject to the whims and dictates of this beautiful creature. He returned her kisses and caresses, and felt every inch of her soft, pliant body as it surged against his, urging him on.

When the moment was exactly right, he moved into her, helped by her cool hands and long, supple fingers. He pushed against her unbelievably wet softness. Le raked his back with her nails and for a moment Mike was afraid he would lose control, but he managed to hang on, to match his rhythm to hers, allowing her time to reach her own pinnacle. Then, as he felt her melting into white-hot fire beneath him, he allowed his own body to erupt into a shattering climax.

Afterward they lay together for several moments, neither moving nor speaking. But the feel of her skin and the scent of her musk reawakened his ardor. He went to her and they made love a second time.

This time Mike had no difficulty in controlling himself, and it was slower and even more sensual. When they finished they lay in each other's arms and Mike thought of how it had been with her. It was exotic and exciting, and his head spun with the dizziness of it. They had asked nothing from each other, save the momentary truth of sexual pleasure, and in that they had given as much as they had received.

Colonel Mot sipped his drink quietly and looked through the large window into the bedroom at his wife and the American helicopter pilot. The glass through which Mot was looking was actually a one-way mirror, which in Le's bedroom was the mirror on her ornate dresser.

Mot felt a fluttering in the pit of his stomach, a slight weakness at the back of his knees, and a dampness in the palms of his hands. His breath came in short, ragged gasps, and there was a pounding erection pushing at the front of his pants. It was always this way when he watched his wife having sex with another man, or with other women.

Theirs was an accommodating arrangement, he thought. She enjoyed sex, and had been wonderfully cooperative over the idea of having a one-way glass installed in the bedroom so that Mot could watch anytime he wished. As soon as he learned of Le's infatuation with the American pilot, he had urged her to find some way to bring him over. It was for that reason that he asked to present an award personally. That, and the "reception," was all it took to get him here. And now, it was well worth it.

The arrangement between Mot and his wife wasn't all one-way. He allowed her to enjoy sex with other men, and women, while she allowed him to indulge in his own particular tastes.

"Colonel, do you wish to make love now?" a voice asked from behind him.

Mot turned toward the sound of the voice. There, standing by the bed behind him, was a beautiful young girl . . . a very young girl.

"Yes," Mot said thickly. He went to the girl's bed and stood there as her experienced young hands removed his clothes. When he was totally naked, the girl lay down, then looked up at him, waiting expectantly.

Across town, Ernie made Olympic circles on the table in the bar of the Hotel Caravel. The Caravel was Saigon's most elegant bar and hotel. Many of the TV reporters had suites there. Ernie had a low-rent apartment down on Le Loi, but he sometimes came here for dinner and drinks. He didn't come here too often, though, because he was disgusted with the phoniness of the correspondents who stood around in neatly tailored jungle fatigues, telling lies of their adventures. Often one reporter's lie would end up in another reporter's story.

"Hello. May I join you?" A soft female voice came from behind him.

Ernie started to wave her away. She was one of the Vietnamese bar girls. She was an exceptionally beautiful woman, and, like all the Caravel women, very cultured. But she was a whore, no different, except for her price, from the whores who worked the doorways and corners of "100 P Alley."

Ernie hesitated for a moment. Then he thought: *Why not?* Who the hell did he have to be faithful to? He had never found the right woman to make marriage work. There was no reason for him to hold back. He smiled at the girl, and her hesitant smile deepened. She sat at his table.

"I'll get a room," Ernie said.

"You don't want to have a drink first?" the woman asked.

"I'll buy a bottle of champagne," Ernie said. "We can take it with us."

"Oh, champagne! What are we celebrating?"

"A friend of mine got an award today," he said. "And if my suspicions are right, he wound up getting more than he ever thought he would."

"I don't understand."

"It doesn't matter. Come along, let's get the champagne and a room."

A few moments later, Ernie was standing at the large, tinted window in the room on the seventh floor. From here he could look out over the Saigon River, and in the evening sun, the river gleamed like molten gold.

"It's pretty from up here," Ernie said, "where you can't smell it, or see the turds floating in it."

"Why do you talk that way?" the woman asked from the bed behind him. "I thought you bought champagne to be happy."

Ernie turned toward the bed and saw her lying there, totally nude, waiting for him. She was on her side, and her head was propped up on her elbow. Her other arm was resting on her bare skin, with her hand at her hip. Her fingers seemed to be gracefully inviting him to the center of her charms. Ernie smiled at her and walked over to the bed. He began taking off his own clothes.

"Honey, if a man saw someone like you waiting in his bed and he wasn't happy, I'd say there was something seriously wrong with him."

The woman laughed, then lay on her back and raised her arms to him.

Ernie reached over and turned off the light as he went to her. Without the lamp, there was only the soft, golden light of sunset, and the image of the girl on the bed with him softened in the shadows.

Ernie looked into the girl's eyes and saw they were half closed, like almonds, shielded by lashes of delicate lace, and he wondered why anyone so beautiful would be in such a profession. He bent his head to hers and their lips met. Her teeth nibbled against his bottom lip, and her tongue teased his.

She guided him into her and they made love, slowly and sensously, until he felt himself approaching the pinnacle. He forced himself back, holding on to the delicious agony of the quest. Finally he heard the girl beneath him take several sharp gasps. Then he felt her quiver, and her hands gripped his back. She let out a long sigh, and when she did, he surrendered himself to the white heat that had been pulling at him for several moments. He felt himself slipping down through space, drained of all sensation save the connecting flesh and splash of seminal fluid. And the rush of white heat that blotted out everything.

# Chapter Seven

Ernie watched the aircraft coming back from their mission. They banked low around the 605th DS shed, then followed in a long line, finally breaking off to hover over the individual pads. He drove the borrowed Jeep out to the ship he knew Mike was flying, then got out and stood in the hot breath of jet fumes as Mike killed the engine. He walked up to the pilot's door and saw Mike filling out the logbook.

"How'd it go?" Ernie asked.

"It's a bitch out there," Mike answered. He took off his flight helmet, leaving his sweat-dampened hair plastered to his forehead. "They moved some anti-aircraft guns onto Widow's Peak."

"Widow's Peak?"

"Yeah. I don't know what it's really called; it's a hill about thirty minutes northeast of here, right at the entrance to Di Shau Valley. We've been working that area for the last month with no problem. Then today, right out of the blue, they opened up on us with flak. They got two ships."

"I'm sorry to hear that."

"Move the chicken plate for me, will you?"

"Yeah, sure," Ernie said. He opened the pilot's door, then slid the armored plate back so Mike could get out.

"What are you doing up here?" Mike asked.

"Hopped a ride up this morning," Ernie said. "Thought I might come up with an idea for a story, but nothing yet. Now, I'm looking for a ride back to Saigon."

"If the evening distribution hasn't gone yet, I'll take you back," Mike said. "You still owe me a dinner."

"You're on," Ernie agreed.

"Mr. Carmack, Colonel Todaro wants to see you," someone called.

"Shit! Wonder what he wants," Mike said.

"Want a ride over to his office?" Ernie offered. "I borrowed Sergeant Pohl's Jeep to come out to the flight line."

"Sure," Mike said. He carried his flak jacket and helmet over to the Jeep, then tossed it in the back. Ernie slid in under the wheel and they started across the airfield toward Colonel Todaro's headquarters.

They drove by a row of cut-down fifty-five-gallon oil drums along the edge of the runway where half a dozen Vietnamese women, under the watchful eye of Specialist Schuler, were pouring diesel fuel into the drums. The drums had been pulled from the outdoor toilets, and they were called honey buckets. Every day the honey buckets would be burned off and the foul-smelling smoke would drift over the compound. No part of the camp would escape the odor, not even the mess tents where the men ate.

Beyond Schuler's mama-sans was the 605th Maintenance Company, and there, on the perforated steel planking, sat several helicopters in various stages of assembly. It was this company that would send a helicopter into the field to recover those helicopters that had either crashed or been shot down. The recovery crew was known as Goodnature 3, and Ernie once did a story about them. The V.C. knew that any downed helicopter would bring the recovery crew in, so they often set ambushes for them.

Colonel Todaro's headquarters, a newly installed Quonset hut, was on the other side of the field hospital. As Ernie drove by the hospital he saw two Dustoff Hueys sitting on the pads out front. Both had been used to evacuate the air crews of the two helicopters that were shot down by anti-aircraft fire from Widow's Peak. He also saw a couple of bikini-clad nurses lying on a blanket in front of the hospital, sunning themselves. Ernie watched a three-quarter-ton truck loaded with E.M. turn around and drive back slowly to enjoy a second look.

The sign outside the headquarters building read: CLEAR YOUR WEAPONS HERE. An arrow pointed to a fifty-five-gallon drum full of sand. Ernie had no weapon to clear, but Mike slipped the magazine from his .45, jacked the barrel back to clear the chamber, then pulled the trigger with the gun pointed into the sand.

"Oh, Mr. Carmack, just a minute," Sergeant Pohl said. "I'll tell Colonel Todaro you're here."

"Thanks," Mike said.

A moment later Colonel Todaro appeared, and seeing Ernie, he invited him into his office as well.

"You might as well get in on this now," he said. "After all, we do have to keep the folks back home informed, don't we?"

"We try to, Colonel," Ernie said, following the two men into Colonel Todaro's office. Todaro indicated they should have a seat.

"Captain Wilson came back with the first element and gave me a full report. I know we lost two helicopters," Todaro said.

"Yes, sir."

"What happened?"

"There were anti-aircraft guns at Widow's Peak. They opened up on us, taking us completely by surprise. They must have moved them in during the night. They weren't there before."

Todaro sighed and rubbed his cheek, then looked at Mike. "Those guns are going to cause us a lot of trouble," he said. "A great deal of trouble."

"They don't have to," Mike said.

"What do you mean?"

"We know where they are now. All we have to do is avoid them."

"We can't avoid them."

"Why the hell not?"

"Because, Mr. Carmack, in three days we're going to put two battalions of troops into Di Shau Valley. There's an entire V.C. regiment in there, and we're going to wipe them out."

"Colonel, if the V.C. are in there, let them stay in there," Mike said. "What the hell harm are they doing? We have no supply routes through there and they can't operate as an effective unit from there without coming out through the mouth. Looks to me like we've got them bottled up. We ought to just keep them there."

"They can slip out a few at a time," Colonel Todaro said. "Mr. Carmack, you know how this war is. It's a rare opportunity when we can get so many V.C. in one spot. We must take advantage of it when we can."

"When we can," Mike said. "It's no accident they are in there. They know we can't come after them without going through the mouth of the valley. And that we can't do that as long as the guns are in place."

"Then we must take them out," Colonel Todaro suggested.

"How?"

"The same way we took out the guns at Binh Loi. Take them head on."

"No, sir."

"What do you mean?"

"This isn't the same situation we had at Binh Loi," Mike explained. "There we had all kinds of maneuverability against the guns. We could come at them from any direction we wanted . . . we could even evade their fire. But at Widow's Peak the guns are right inside the valley mouth, and the only way to hit them is straight on. That means they know where we're coming from, and how high we'll be. They also know how fast we'll be flying . . . which, believe me, isn't fast enough.''

"Nevertheless, those guns have to be taken out,'' Colonel Todaro said. "And I was hoping you would volunteer for the mission.''

"Colonel, what made you think I'd volunteer?''

"Well, after all, Mr. Carmack, you are our most experienced pilot.''

"Yes, sir,'' Mike answered.

"So?''

"Colonel, how do you think I got to be the most experienced? You've heard the story, there are bold pilots and there are old pilots, but there are no old bold pilots. I intend to be old.''

"That's too bad,'' Todaro said. "I'm sure I could get Captain Bailey to volunteer to lead the mission.''

"Bailey? Colonel, you aren't serious. Hell, he's only been flying a year.''

"Nevertheless, he is a dedicated officer who realizes where his duty lies.''

"Goddammit! Colonel, there's nothing in the book that says a man's duty is to commit suicide. Unless you're planning on starting your own Kamikaze unit.''

"There have always been dangerous missions, Mr. Carmack,'' Todaro said. "And there have always been men dedicated enough and brave enough to take them on.''

"Look, why don't you just ask for an air force strike? They can slip a couple of jets in there, burn the shit out of it with napalm, and that'll be all there is to it.''

"No," Todaro said. "I don't intend to give the air force the satisfaction of coming to our aid the first time we have an air strike that's a little tough."

"Coming to our aid? Goddammit! Colonel, that's what the hell we have the air force for! That's what they do for a living."

"And I'm trying to get it through your head that this is also what we do for a living," Todaro said.

"If we try that, some of us are going to wind up dying for a living," Mike replied. "Especially if you have Bailey lead the mission."

"Suppose I lead the mission," Todaro suggested. "I have almost as many hours as you. Would you give the mission a better chance of success if I led it?"

"A little better, yes, sir," Mike agreed.

"All right, Mr. Carmack, I'll make a deal with you. You volunteer for the mission, and I'll lead it. Otherwise, it'll be Bailey and anyone he can get to volunteer."

"Every low-time pilot in the goddamned unit will volunteer for it, Colonel, you know that. They're all a bunch of gung-ho bastards who have no idea what they'd be getting into."

"Then you volunteer," Todaro said. "And you select the team from among the other volunteers. I'll lead it and we'll take those guns out."

"You've got me by the balls, Colonel, and I don't like that," Mike said.

"You know what they say, Mr. Carmack — grab them by their balls, and their hearts and minds will come along."

"All right, I'll do it."

"I thought you might see it my way."

"I want to take the distribution run to Saigon," Mike said. "I want to give Mr. Chapel a ride back."

"All right," Todaro agreed. "I don't know who we have scheduled for it, but you can take the flight."

"Thanks," Mike said.

Half an hour later they took off over the roof of the DS shed. Mike kept the nose low to build up air speed, then pulled up on the collective to gain altitude. He leveled off at 2,500 and called Paris Control, the central flight controller at Tan Son Nhut.

"Paris Control, Gunslinger 501 out of Phu Loi for Tan Son Nhut, 2,500 in a UH-1B."

"Gunslinger 501, squawk flash."

Mike punched the sqawk button on his transponder.

"Roger, Gunslinger 501, we have you. Be advised we have artillery in Tango-Papa and Charley-Charley coordinates, rounds at 7,500 feet."

"Roger, Paris 501, out."

Ernie looked through the window at the lush green jungle below them, split by the winding and shining Saigon River, and interspersed with flooded rice paddies and fields of all colors from black through brown, yellow through green. Little villages sat clustered along the banks of the river, or along the concrete ribbon that was Highway 13. Dozens of yellow-and-blue buses moved, antlike, along the highway, competing with the trucks and Jeeps for right of way. From up here it seemed impossible that the peaceful-looking land they were flying over was at war.

Finally the sprawling, teeming city of Saigon came into view, and Mike released the friction lock to lower the pitch. The blades began popping as they spilled air, and the helicopter started a very gradual descent, until they were about two hundred feet above a cluster of antennae and heading straight for the helicopter landing area.

"Paris Control, Gunslinger 501 over antenna farm," Mike said.

"Gunslinger 501, clear to land at pilot's discretion."

Mike clicked his mike button twice in acknowledgment, then continued on down, terminating his approach about three feet off the ground. He hovered to set down on the landing pad indicated by one of the flight line personnel, then killed the engine.

"All right," he said. "Where do you want to take me to feed me? Bear in mind I have to be back here in an hour and a half at the most."

"There's a Mexican place on base called the Casa Grande. It's damned good. Want to try it?"

"Sure. Why not?"

"Okay. This way, Pancho, follow," Ernie said, mimicking the old Cisco Kid movies.

"Oh, Cisco," Mike replied.

The Casa Grande was operated by the air force NCO club, but was open to men and women of all ranks and all branches of service. It was long and narrow, with red-and-white-checkered tablecloths and authentic Mexican food.

"Mike," Ernie asked as he lifted a taco to his mouth, "you really going to go through with that crazy mission?"

"If I don't, that asshole will have Bailey and a bunch of kids try it," Mike said. "It would be a slaughter."

"You think you'll have any better chance?"

"I've got enough sense to know that it can't be done, so I don't intend to do anything crazy," Mike said. He sighed. "And if Todaro goes along, maybe he'll see that, too, and call the shit off."

"I wouldn't count on that," Ernie said. "I've known people like Todaro before."

"Yeah," Mike said. "Me too." He smiled. "You want to go with me?"

"On this mission?" Ernie asked. "Are you crazy?"

"I just thought you might want to do a story on it, that's all."

"I'll wait on the ground," Ernie said. "You can tell me all about it when you get back."

Left unsaid was what both of them thought. *If* he got back.

# Chapter Eight

"I want you to fly in the five slot," Todaro told Mike. Command was six, second-in-command was five. It was highly unusual for a warrant officer to fly as command or second-in-command. It was even more unusual if there were commissioned officers involved in the operation.

"You don't think that'll cause any trouble with the captains and lieutenants?" Mike asked.

"Captains Wilson and Bailey have agreed to go along with it," Todaro said. "I don't anticipate any trouble from the one or two lieutenants we'll have. I imagine most of the element will be made up of warrants anyway. We do want our most experienced people."

"That's true," Mike said. He looked at the map

of Di Shau Valley. "What have you got worked up?"

"Here are the air-recon photos," Todaro said, opening a manila folder. "We've had Mohawks over the area several times. Now, look, do you see this stream? It winds through here, then goes right up into the valley here. I intend to come in on the deck, following the stream bed right up to the guns. They won't even know we're there until we're in the valley."

"But, Colonel, once we're in the valley, we have nowhere to go except straight ahead, then up. We'll be sitting ducks for at least twenty seconds."

"Just twenty seconds," Todaro said.

"Twenty seconds is an eternity when you're in the hot seat. If you don't know how long it can be, put your finger in a candle flame for twenty seconds."

"Obviously a mission of this nature is not without its risks," Todaro said. "But the plan already has approval. Brigade approved it this afternoon."

"If that's the way you want to do it, then that's the way we'll do it," Mike said.

"Do you have another suggestion?"

"Yeah. Let the air force do it."

"I have already told you, Mr. Carmack, this is an army mission, and army aviation will take care of it."

"Yes, sir."

Suddenly Todaro smiled and put his hand on Mike's shoulder.

"Mike, we shouldn't argue over this, you and me. Hell, I remember when you were a brand-new

W-1 right out of flight school and I was a green-assed second lieutenant. We were assigned to Board Six, remember?"

"Yes, sir."

"We tied .30-caliber field-machine guns to the skids of H-13s and jury-rigged a trigger so we could fire them at barrels of sand. Everyone thought we were crazy to arm helicopters, but by God we kept at it. Now we've got whole companies of gunships, and you should see some of the things on the drawing boards! Two-hundred-mile-an-hour helicopters with target acquisition lasers, guided missiles, rapid-firing cannon. It's unbelievable what they have planned."

"Yes, sir, I remember all that," Mike said. "And if we had one of those super models now, I'd feel better about this mission. For all the impact we can have on those guns at Widow's Peak, we may as well be flying those H-13s at Board Six."

"I'm sorry you feel that way," Todaro said. "I'd hoped to have your full support on this mission."

Mike ran his hand through his hair and sighed. "You've got it, Colonel," he said. "I won't say any more about it. By the way, what kind of ordinance are you taking?"

"I thought I'd take rockets."

"A suggestion, sir?"

"What?"

"Put mini-guns on every other ship. Take them in as fire teams at staggered altitudes. The mini-guns might keep Charley's head down while the rockets are doing their job."

Todaro rubbed his chin with his hand and looked

at the photos for a long moment before he answered. "Yeah," he finally agreed. "Yeah, that sounds like a pretty good idea at that. I may just do that."

"I'll see Dick and have him start his maintenance boys on the gun kits. They'll be ready to go when we are," Mike offered.

"Good, good," Todaro said. He smiled broadly. "Cheer up, Mike. After this mission your friend Ernie will really have something to write about."

"Yes, sir," Mike said.

"Well, what say we get started?"

Back in Saigon, Ernie received a surprise telephone call. The caller was Madam Mot, and she asked Ernie if he would like to take her to Phu Cuong to visit an orphanage that she sponsored.

"Or do you wish to write only the bad things about us?" she added.

"No, of course I don't want to write only the bad things," Ernie answered.

"Good. Meet me at the Continental in one half hour," she said, hanging up before Ernie could reply.

"What was that all about?" Ben Adams asked. Ben was with Associated Press and had dropped by CPI to visit.

"That was Madam Mot," Ernie answered. "She wants me to take her to Phu Cuong."

"Sure she does." Ben chuckled. "And Madam Ky wants me to take her to Vung Tau. Okay, hide your stories from me, see if I give a damn."

Ernie reached for his hat.

"Are you really going to leave? I mean, just like that?"

"Just like that," Ernie said.

"Okay, just wait and see how I treat you when you come to visit me."

"You didn't come to visit, Ben you came to borrow."

"Oh, yeah, I did, didn't I? What about it? Can I use your Johnny Mathis tapes tonight? I'm tellin' you, this kid is one good-looking round eye, the kind that you need to loosen up with the two Johnnys — Johnny Mathis and Johnny Walker."

"Take it," Ernie said. "But I refuse to be held responsible for the consequences."

"Thanks. I'll give you a complete report. Oh, and do tell me all about Madam Mot, will you?"

Ernie checked out a Jeep from the press pool and drove over to the Continental Hotel. The Continental was an example of one of the fine blends of culture in the city. It occupied a busy corner in the heart of Saigon, and an open veranda afforded customers the luxury of sitting quietly over a drink or a meal while they watched the people of the city pass by. Overhead fans turned briskly, while white-jacketed waiters darted about carrying gin-and-tonics and other cooling drinks balanced on serving trays.

Ernie parked in front of the hotel and pulled the locking chain through the steering wheel to secure the Jeep. An old man shuffled by, long wisps of white hair protruding from his chin to form a beard that waved in the gentle breeze. He clasped his palms together and dipped his hands several times in a position of respect. Ernie returned the gesture.

Ernie chose a table to wait for Madam Mot. He would have preferred a table right at the entrance, but it was occupied by a man he recognized as the Minister of Imports. The Minister of Imports was reading a newspaper, and the fat, sausagelike fingers of both hands were adorned with diamond rings. A gold Rolex was on one wrist. Rolls of flesh from his thick neck lay in layers across the silk collar of his expensive suit.

Ernie took a seat, ordered a beer, and waited. A few moments later a taxi pulled to a stop at the curb and Ernie watched as a woman sitting in the shadows of the back seat passed money across to the driver. When she stepped out of the car, Ernie recognized her as Madam Mot. He walked over to meet her.

"Thank you for coming," she said. "Have you a car?"

"A Jeep," Ernie said. "I hope you don't mind."

"Heavens, no. I think riding in a Jeep is great fun."

Ernie led her over to the Jeep. Then when she was seated, he walked around to his side to unlock the chain.

"You say we are going to an orphanage?"

"Yes, at Phu Cuong," Madam Mot said. "It's near Phu Loi."

"I know."

"Mr. Carmack is at Phu Loi, isn't he?" Madam Mot asked.

"Yes."

"Perhaps you can go see him . . . deliver a message for me."

"Deliver a message for you?"

"Yes. Tell him my sister has a house in My Tho. I will meet him there this Sunday."

Ernie looked surprised as he started the Jeep. She smiled at him.

"Didn't Mr. Carmack tell you?"

"Tell me what?"

"We have been intimate."

Ernie coughed. "No," he said. "He didn't tell me."

"I would have thought he would have spread it everywhere by now," she said matter-of-factly.

The drive to Phu Cuong was quite pleasant once they crossed the river and the congestion of Saigon was behind them. Highway 13 wound through lush green fields and quiet little villages. Brilliant splashes of color lined the road where flowers grew in profusion.

Phu Cuong sat on a bend in the river about fifteen miles north of Saigon. It supplied fish to the markets of all nearby hamlets, and the fishmongers of the hamlets came to town every day to buy. They walked along the bank of the river and poked through the catch, which, when laid out, stretched for almost a quarter of a mile.

To the American, the smell was very strong, but to the Phu Cuong resident the smell was just part of the excitement. The market was the center of great activity. In addition to the customers and vendors, there were also the passengers of the bus line and the ferry service, both of which used the market as a terminal.

The orphanage to which they went was badly understaffed and overpopulated. Ernie followed Madam Mot around the grounds while she visited with the children and conducted business with the director. She introduced him to everyone and he recorded their names so that when he wrote the story their names would be correct.

As Ernie walked around he became the center of attention to every child in the institution. They laughed and shouted to one another, and pulled at the hair on his arms. To the children, most Americans were soldiers they saw driving by in Jeeps, trucks, or personnel carriers. In Ernie, they had the opportunity to look at an American, a *My*, up close, and they were taking every advantage to do so.

"You can go now," Madam Mot said. "I'll keep myself occupied right here until you return."

"They're comin' back!" someone shouted. And Ernie, who had been sitting in the pilots' lounge, hurried out toward the landing pads.

Ernie could feel the beat of the engines and blades of the approaching helicopters, and he looked north as they approached. There was something wrong! He looked toward Sergeant Pohl with an expression of confusion on his face.

"I thought you told me thirteen ships went out."

"Yes, sir, that's what I have on my board," Pohl said. "Thirteen."

"Well, has one element already landed?"

"No, sir," Pohl answered.

"But there are only five in this group. I wonder why they're coming back in two groups."

"Beats the hell out of me, Mr. Chapel," Pohl said. "I'm only the operations sergeant. I don't know why the hell anyone does anything over here."

The Hueys approached in a single file over the 605th DS shed, then broke left for the final approach to the landing pads. Ernie watched them as they hovered by. To the casual observer each helicopter looked exactly alike, but there was a slightly different personality to each ship and Ernie had already learned to identify the one flown by Mike Carmack. He saw it . . . but he didn't see Rindell's aircraft.

"They must've broken up into two elements," Pohl said. "Captain Bailey isn't with them; he must be in command of the second group."

"Yeah," Ernie said. "I guess that's where Rindell is."

The five Hueys sat down lightly on the pads and the pilots killed the engines. Now the whine was replaced by the swooshing noise of the rotors as they began spinning down. The gunners and crew chiefs hopped out, began opening the doors and sliding back the chicken plates. Ernie saw Mike get out and walk slowly toward him.

"Where's the other group?" Ernie asked when Mike was close enough.

Mike looked up at Ernie. "What other group?" he asked. A sudden knot formed in Ernie's stomach. He felt a dizzying wave of nausea. "My God, Mike! You don't mean this is all that's coming back?"

"Yeah," Mike said quietly. "John Rindell's dead. So is Peters, Walls, Throgmorton . . . three-fourths of the men in my tent. We lost eight ships today. I don't know how many were killed."

"What . . . what happened?"

"You know what it would be like if you put a bird in a food blender? That's what it was like today. I'm not surprised we lost eight ships. I'm surprised that five of us came back."

"What about the guns you went after?"

"We didn't even come close."

"I'm sorry, Mike," Ernie said. It was a weak statement, but under the circumstances, it was all he could come up with.

"I'm going to get drunk," Mike said. "Not at the pilots' lounge; there's not enough liquor there. I'm going to the club. Care to come along?"

"The club isn't even open, is it?"

"We'll open it," Mike promised. He started straight for the club, followed closely by the quiet, solemn-faced pilots from the other ships. Only Todaro remained behind; he had not emerged from his helicopter.

Ernie watched Mike and the others walk slowly toward the club; he looked back toward the helicopters. By now every blade was still, and the crew chiefs were tying down the ships. The ground crews for the helicopters that hadn't yet returned were standing around in shocked silence.

Ernie stood on the perforated steel planking alone, looking toward Todaro's ship. He knew that Todaro had insisted upon this mission, despite protests from Mike and everyone else with any experience.

"Get out of that helicopter, you son of a bitch," he said under his breath. "You've got to get out of there sometime. You can't stay there the rest of the day."

Finally, Ernie decided to walk over there. As he got closer he could see the damage it and the other helicopters had sustained. There were dozens of holes in the tail cone and blades. The others had the same degree of damage. It would be several days before they were patched well enough to fly again.

Ernie stood about fifty feet away, looking at Todaro. Todaro just sat there with a strange, almost detached expression on his face. Finally he noticed Ernie looking at him, and, as his chicken plate had already been pulled back, he got out.

"What happened, Colonel?" Ernie asked.

"We ran out of ammunition," Todaro answered.

Ernie ran his hand through his hair and looked at the empty pads. "Looks to me like you damned near ran out of men," he replied.

"It was rough," Todaro said, not really reacting to Ernie's comment. "It was really rough."

Todaro walked right by Ernie, moving in a slow, shocked shuffle. Ernie knew that it would do no good to shout at him, or accuse him of leading good men to a useless death. At this very moment, Todaro was barely aware that Ernie was even there. Ernie watched him until he walked between the maintenance hangar and the operations shack, then disappeared behind a row of tents.

"I wish I could write this story," he said quietly. "If there was ever any one story that is symbolic of this entire war, it is this one. That's exactly how I would lose my accreditation if I wrote it. But someday, Colonel. Someday, after this war is over, and the Vietnam vet is a vague memory from a forgotten war, I'm going to tell what happened here today."

When Ernie stepped into the officers' club a few minutes later, he could smell the food being prepared for lunch. The tables were set with tablecloths, silver, and napkins, while in the darkened bar area the nine pilots who returned, eight warrant officers and one captain, had pulled a couple of unset tables together. Open whiskey bottles sat on the table before them, and they were all drinking quietly.

"There!" a Vietnamese voice said. "That's them. I told them, 'No drink before 1600!' But they no listen. They come behind bar and get bottles anyway."

The voice belonged to the Vietnamese civilian who had been hired to oversee the other Vietnamese employees of the club. He was talking to the club officer.

The club officer, a lieutenant, stepped over to the table. "Here, you men, what do you think you're doing?" he demanded.

"What the hell does it look like we're doing, you dumb shit?" Mike replied. He drained the rest of his glass, then wiped his mouth with the back of his hand. "We're drinkin'."

"You can't drink in here until 1600 hours!"

"Let it go, Lieutenant," Ernie said quietly.

The lieutenant looked around and saw Ernie, in uniform, but wearing a press patch.

"I will not let it go," the lieutenant said. "These men have no —"

"Throw the son of a bitch out," Captain Wilson said. Besides Colonel Todaro, Captain Wilson was the only surviving commissioned officer from the mission.

The two warrants at the end of the table nearest the lieutenant stood up and grabbed him under the arms, then dragged him across the floor and tossed him through the door.

"I'll be back!" the lieutenant called. "Just wait! I'll be back with the provost marshal!"

Ernie walked over to sit in a chair offered him by Mike. He looked at the men and saw a closeness between them that, at that moment, was closer than any relationship in the world. There was no love that could compare with this; not the love of a man for a woman, not the love of a man for his family or country. It was a private love, shared only by those who had been in the crucible of battle, and understood by no one but them.

"I'll say this for Todaro," one of the warrants said. "He's got guts."

"Guts, hell. He's crazy."

"What happened?" Ernie asked.

"Todaro was the first one in," Mike said. "He had the rockets. Rindell went in with the mini-guns to cover him. Rindell got hit right off. He must've taken an explosive round in the fuel cell because his ship just blew up. I figured Todaro would break off his run, but he didn't. He went right on in. It was all a waste. His rockets burst on the rock wall of the mountain."

"The next two to go in went down," someone

else said. "Then Joe and I went in, with Ollie and Fergus in the mini-gun ship. By then it was so hot that all I could think of was getting the hell out of there. We fired, but it didn't do anything."

"It kept going like that," Mike went on. "On the first pass we lost five. Five, on one pass! I thought for sure he would break off and come back; hell, it was obvious we couldn't do anything. But Todaro ordered another pass. This time I figured I'd make sure it was our last pass, so I fired off everything we had left. We lost three that time. Then I heard Todaro order a third pass. I thought, the crazy bastard! He's just going to keep going until we're all gone!"

"What happened?"

"Like me, everyone else had fired everything on their first two passes. So, Todaro didn't have any choice but to order us home."

"What I'm wondering about is, what happens now?" Captain Wilson said.

"What do you mean?" Mike asked.

"You may not have noticed it, Mike, but we don't have a company left. Our exec, most of our pilots, and damned near all of our aircraft are gone. What happens now? Are we going to be broken up and sent to new companies, or what?"

"I don't know about the rest of you guys," one man said. "But I ain't leavin'."

"Amen to that, brother," another said.

At that moment, the club officer returned. This time his attitude was totally changed.

"I'm sorry, guys," he said. "I didn't know what

happened. Drink all you want . . . the club'll take care of it.''

Mike smiled. ''Lieutenant, there's hope for you yet.''

# Chapter Nine

In My Tho on Sunday morning, Le got up with the sun and walked through the quiet house, picking her way carefully through the sleepers whose straw mats were strewn about on the floor. She stood on the open porch and looked out toward the Mekong. A soft breeze blowing off the river carried with it a fish smell that was somehow reassuring . . . as if reminding Le of the timelessness of Vietnam.

The fishermen of the village had already gone out, and their flat boats glided effortlessly through the still water, the reflection of the painted eyes on the boats glaring back from the mirrored surface. The clacks of the wooden blocks the fishermen slapped together to attract the fish rolled across the water with a rhythmic, almost musical quality.

Most of the pre-dawn mist had been burned

away by the red disk of the rising sun, but enough remained to clothe the scene in a diaphanous haze, making it appear as if the village were a painting on silk in pastel blues, purples, and rose.

As the morning shadows lightened, Le became aware that she was not alone on the porch. The father of her sister's husband was also there. He was sitting quietly at the other end, looking at Le with deep, dark eyes.

"The sunrise is very beautiful," Le said, startled by his presence and speaking merely to overcome her awkwardness.

The old man didn't answer.

"I was unable to sleep," she added.

Still no answer.

"It was hot, and I came for a breath of fresh air." Le was very uncomfortable, and the more she tried to cover her embarrassment, the more obvious it became.

"You are troubled by the American," the old man said, finally speaking.

"What do you mean?"

"At first, you thought merely to entertain yourself with the American. As long as it was merely for amusement, your husband would allow it. But it is no longer entertainment. You are in love with the American."

Le turned away from the old man and looked out over the water again with tear-dimmed eyes.

"You are old and wise. Tell me, why is such a thing to be? Why must my heart be filled with love for one I cannot have?"

"You ask a question for which I have no answer," the old man said quietly.

"Then what should I do? Should I get a divorce?"

"Again, you have asked a question that I cannot answer."

"What good is it to live so long if you have no wisdom to share?" Le asked in frustrated anger.

"You are a woman of the world and have met many foreigners. In the world of the foreigners, how are such things handled?"

"In America, one can easily get a divorce and marry another. It is frequently done and brings no shame."

"And you would divorce your husband for this American if you could?"

"Yes."

"Such a desire in your heart is a deed done," the old man said. "It is too late for counsel."

The sounds of the others awakening reached the porch. The private conversation between Le and the old man halted, and their relationship changed as abruptly as the closing of a door. He became once again the extra houseguest, the old grandfather waiting to die. And she became the almost feared lady from Saigon, a relative by blood but a stranger by life-style. The temporary bridge they had built between them was gone. It was as if they had never spoken a word this morning. And now there would be no more real communication between them, only superficial conversation. Not even their eyes would exchange an awareness of the brief encounter they had shared.

It was late in the afternoon and the sun was low on the western horizon. The pilot lowered the collective and the helicopter began its descent into My Tho. He looked around toward Mike, who was riding in the back, not his usual place, but he had hitched a ride on a courier flight.

"I'll be back here at seven tomorrow morning, Chief, if you want a ride back," the lieutenant said.

"Thanks," Mike answered. "I'll be here."

Mike walked away from the helicopter and started toward the house where he was to meet Le, following the directions he had written on a sheet of paper. The house was an easy quarter-mile walk from the airfield.

The contrast between the elegant villa where Le lived in Saigon and the home of her sister in My Tho was unbelievable. Her sister's house was built on the river's edge, and the back part of it was on stilts, actually protruding over the water. The house was covered with sheet tin made from pressed soft-drink and beer cans. A naked child sat in the dirt, and others ran alongside Mike, laughing and shouting with excitement.

An old man was sitting on the porch of the house holding a fishing pole. He looked at Mike but didn't speak.

"Are you catching many fish?" Mike asked.

"No," the old man answered. "I have told the fish I do not want trouble with them. I only appear to fish, so that I may sit here and sleep, and the young ones will not say that I am lazy. You are the one called Mike?"

"Yes," Mike answered. "How do you know my name?"

"I am the father of the husband of Le's sister,"

the old man said. "Le has spoken of you. She is waiting now to see you." He pointed to the house.

"Thank you," Mike said.

Mike was met at the door by an old mama-san. Her face had the texture of old leather, and black spittle hung in the wrinkles of her chin.

"I've come to see Madam Mot," Mike said.

The old woman stared at him unblinking, and he would have thought she didn't hear him had she not motioned for him to follow her. He walked through the house to the back. Then she stopped and pointed to a door.

"Is she in there?"

The old woman said something in Vietnamese.

"I don't understand."

The old woman spoke again, and when Mike still didn't understand, she slid the door open and motioned for him to step through. When he was on the other side, she slid the door shut.

Mike stood there for a moment, looking around the room. It was a fairly large room, filled with lacquered furniture, an ornate mirror, a dressing screen, a bed, and a small bedside table. The floor was covered with some type of ceramic tile. He was certain that this was the best room in the house.

Mike heard the musical lilt of Vietnamese being spoken. Then he looked up to see Le enter from another room.

"Mike," she said, smiling. "I am glad you could come. I have food prepared for you."

Mike caught his breath. Le looked completely different from any previous time he had ever seen her. She was wearing an *ao dai*, but not the expensive, richly embroidered kind she usually wore.

This one was pale blue and plain. Her face was scrubbed clean of makeup; her fingernails were unpainted. And yet, he believed he had never seen her more beautiful.

Le led him into another room, where he saw a fully set table. She invited him to sit and he was immediately surrounded by silent shuffling women. From one he received a scented, dampened cloth, from another a beer, and from still another a heaping serving of fried rice.

"Who are all these people?" Mike asked.

"They are the family of my sister," Le said. "They wish to serve. I cannot tell them no. They will be hurt."

By the time they finished their dinner, it was dark. Le invited Mike out on the porch, the same porch where she had stood to watch the sunrise that morning. Out on the river a big cargo boat slipped by, its passage marked by a looming black shadow and two tiny running lamps. Mike could hear a baby crying from inside the boat and he knew that one or more families lived on the vessel all the time.

"I like to come to My Tho," Le said. "It is more peaceful here than in Saigon."

"Yes," Mike agreed.

"Peace," she said. "That word has a good sound. Even when spoken in Vietnamese the word *hoa* sounds like a soft sigh. Will we ever have peace, Mike?"

"I don't know," Mike answered. "I really don't know."

"I think not," Le said. "There are too many

men . . . men like my husband, who must have the war. They don't care who wins or who loses . . . they don't care who is right and who is wrong. They care only that there be a war." She looked at him and smiled. "But," she said, changing the subject and the tone of her voice, "you have come to My Tho to see me, and this is a happy event. One should not talk of unpleasant things in the midst of a happy event."

"No," Mike said. He put his arms around her and pulled her to him, then kissed her. "There are too many other things we can do."

"Come," Le invited, leading him away from the porch and back into the bedroom. A small lamp burned on the dresser, barely pushing the dark out of the room. "Please get undressed, Mike," Le said, "unless you intend to sleep with your clothes on."

Mike looked at her. They had made love before, but that time it was a few stolen moments in the afternoon of a hectic day. Now he was being invited to spend the night with her.

As Mike undressed, Le stepped behind the screen. He could see her only from the shoulders up, but even so, he found her undressing immensely stimulating. There was a balletlike grace to her movements as she undressed behind the screen, and when, at last, her shoulders were completely bare, she reached up to release the ivory comb and let her hair tumble down below the screen. Then, and only then, did she come around to show herself.

"Do you want to —" Mike started, but Le put her finger on his lips.

"No talk now," she said. She put her arms around him and pulled his face to hers in a consuming, almost urgent kiss, grinding her naked body against his. Mike grew dizzy with the musk of her perfume and the intensity of her kiss. A fire ignited inside him and spread with amazing speed throughout his body. "Mike," she murmured from deep in her throat. "My own, sweet Mike."

Mike wasn't aware of moving, but somehow they wound up on the bed, tongue to tongue, naked flesh to naked flesh. His hands moved down her body; he felt her skin pulsate beneath his fingers. He moved his fingers deftly across her stomach, and into the silky growth of hair where he felt her incredible hot wetness. She moved to position her body under his, and he rested on top of her. The electric connection of their bodies shot through him like a bolt of flame. She answered his thrusts by moving up to take in more of him, until their bellies were tightly pressed together. She sucked in sharply, whimpering a little from the pleasure of it, as she raised her legs up, then locked them around him.

Le climaxed first; the tingle began in the soles of her feet, then spread in intensity until she was screaming and groaning with pleasure. Somewhere in the explosion, Mike's own orgasm ignited, and he joined her as wave after wave of pleasure broke over them.

Afterward they both slept.

Mike awoke once in the middle of the night. The moon was shining brightly, sailing high in the velvet sky. A pool of iridescence spilled through the window and onto the bed. Le was bathed in a soft shimmering light.

She was asleep, and breathing softly. Mike reached over gently and put his hand on her naked hip. He could feel the sharpness of her hipbone and the soft yielding of her flesh. The contrasting textures were delightful to his sense of touch. He let his hand rest there, enjoying the feeling of possession, until finally sleep claimed him once again.

# Chapter Ten

Ernie Chapel was Colonel Mot's guest at the opening of the new bridge at the village of Duc Tho. It would be, Colonel Mot insisted, a good story of how the Saigon government was helping its people.

The old bridge had consisted of wood and rope, allowing only foot traffic, bicycles, and carts to cross the small river that separated Highway 13 from the village. No vehicles were allowed on the old bridge. There was another bridge about ten miles downriver for vehicles, and a dirt road that ran back to the village. It had served its purpose without significant problems, until the last rainy season, when a flood destroyed the bridge.

Now, at the request of the Saigon government, the U.S. Army Corps of Engineers had built another bridge. The villagers were pleased, but they had no idea that the bridge replacing the one they lost would be a big steel-and-concrete bridge capable of allowing five-ton trucks to cross. That meant that their village, which had been spared the military traffic — and, consequetly, the fight-ing — could now become embroiled in the war. The villagers were not pleased about that. They weren't pleased at all.

"What do you think, Mr. Chapel?" Colonel Mot asked, pointing to the flag-draped bridge. "It is a wonderful thing we have done for the poor people of Duc Tho, don't you think?"

"Colonel, I've heard that some of the people aren't pleased with this bridge," Ernie said. "I've heard they would have preferred a small bridge, like the one they lost."

"Ah . . . they are peasants, unable to think of the future of their village," Colonel Mot said. "Pay no attention to them."

"But didn't you just say that this bridge was built for them? Surely you are interested in what they want?"

"A child does not like to take medicine, but it is good for him," Colonel Mot said. "Perhaps these villagers don't want this bridge now, but it is good for them, and in the long run they will be glad."

"Why don't you let them decide that?"

"Mr. Chapel, you have been in my country for a long time now. You have written stories about our struggle. Surely you, better than any other out-sider, can understand our unique problems. Viet-nam is divided into two classes of people. There are those of us who, by the results of our own in-itiative, are the leaders, while the others, by their sloth and laziness, are the followers. Obviously to such people abstract thoughts of the future are not possible. These people don't really know what they want, so it is up to us to tell them.''

"So much for the principles of democratic reform," Ernie noted.

Colonel Mot, who was already smoking, lit another cigarette from the butt of his old one, then flipped the old one away. Half a dozen children ran to the discarded cigarette butt to fight over it.

"Please, do not misunderstand," Colonel Mot said. "We are for democratic reform, but first I think we must create a society stable enough to accept democracy."

"That's the same thing all dictatorships say," Ernie said.

Colonel Mot laughed and wagged his finger back and forth at Ernie. "Ah, but at least we are not a Communist dictatorship, and right now, as far as your government is concerned, that's all that's important."

"Yes," Ernie agreed reluctantly. "I'm afraid you're right."

"Tell me about Mr. Carmack," Colonel Mot said, changing the subject so sharply that, for a moment, Ernie didn't follow him.

"What?"

"Carmack," Colonel Mot said again. "Your friend, the American pilot."

"What about him?"

"He is fucking my wife."

"Colonel, that's quite an accusation to make," Ernie stammered, but Mot held up his hand to interrupt him.

"I know that he is fucking her, Mr. Chapel. And, within the guidelines I laid out for my wife, I am willing to accept that."

"Guidelines?" Ernie asked with a puzzled expression on his face.

Mot laughed. "I don't expect you to understand," he said. "My wife and I agreed long ago that our relationship wouldn't be limited by conventional restraints. But there were certain guidelines that we agreed to follow, and she isn't following them. She went to My Tho, and I have it on very good authority that Mr. Carmack visited her there."

"I . . . uh . . . am sorry," Ernie said, not knowing what else to say.

"It isn't your fault, or your problem," Colonel Mot said. "I was merely letting you know that I am aware of the situation. Ah, the ceremony is about to begin. Shall we let the subject of my wife's infidelities lie, for the moment?"

"Yes, of course," Ernie said, glad the subject was changed. He had no wish to discuss Madam Mot's extramarital affairs with her husband.

The band from the Vietnamese Army was dressed in starched khaki uniforms with gleaming silver helmet liners and white Sam Browne belts. At the signal from their director they raised their instruments and began to play.

To pay honor to the Americans for building the bridge, the first song the band played was the "Star-Spangled Banner." Despite Ernie's uneasiness over participating in what he felt was an affront to the villagers, he still felt the same thrill he always did at hearing the national anthem.

With an amazing sense of ironic coincidence, the

first explosions on the bridge went off just as the anthem reached the part of "bombs bursting in air." The first bomb was followed by a series of explosions, as the entire bridge went up in smoke. The villagers screamed, and the dignitaries who were standing ready to cut the ribbons dived for cover, along with the soldiers and members of the band.

Ernie watched from the reviewing stand. He was far enough away from the explosions not to be in any personal danger from flying debris, but close enough to watch with morbid fascination as the bridge slowly crumpled, then fell into the water, a useless pile of twisted metal and broken concrete.

The smoke was still hanging in the air when a soldier reported to Colonel Mot. The soldier spoke in Vietnamese, but Ernie had been in the country long enough to understand what he said.

"Colonel, did he say the sappers have been trapped?"

"Yes," Colonel Mot answered. "We had patrols all around here, anticipating something like this."

"You mean you knew the bridge was going to be blown?"

"We received some letters that threatened to do so," Colonel Mot said. He smiled. "Now it seems as if our V.C. friends have been . . . what is the quaint English saying? 'Hoisted by their own petard'? Come. Would you like to go with us?"

"Yes," Ernie said.

Ernie followed Colonel Mot to a nearby Jeep, and seconds later they were roaring down the road with a rooster tail of dust flying behind them. Less than a mile from the edge of the village they saw an armored personnel carrier and another Jeep. Three dozen Vietnamese soldiers were standing in a semicircle around four young Vietnamese men. None of the young men was armed, nor did any of them wear an armband or anything else that would suggest they were V.C. One of the four had been shot and he was being supported by two of the others. His stomach was bright red with blood, and as Ernie looked at him, he realized that the young man was going to die quickly if he didn't get medical attention soon.

"Colonel, that man needs a medic," Ernie said.

"That man is one of the ones who just blew up our bridge," Colonel Mot answered. "He will be attended to when he answers the questions we have for him."

"Colonel, you can't deny him medical attention," Ernie insisted.

"I suppose you will write about the cruelty of the Vietnamese government if I do?"

"There's always that possibility," Ernie said.

"Very well, Mr. Chapel, if it will make you feel better, I will see to his wounds." Mot paused for a moment. Then he laughed, a low, evil laugh. "And then I will have him executed."

Colonel Mot called to one of his officers, and a couple of men took the wounded man over to one of the Jeeps.

"Thank you, Colonel," Ernie started. "I think you will find that —"

Ernie's comment was suddenly interrupted by an explosion. He looked over toward the Jeep where the wounded man had been taken. A puff of smoke hung over the Jeep, but where the wounded man had been there was now nothing but a pile of bloody rags. He had managed to set off a grenade just as the medics bent over to help him. He'd killed himself and the two Vietnamese medics.

"Oh, my God," Ernie said.

Colonel Mot laughed as if it were the greatest joke he had ever heard. Ernie looked at him, shocked that anyone could laugh at such a moment.

"Oh, come now, Mr. Chapel," Colonel Mot said. "Don't look at me like that. The blood of those men is on your hands. You are the one who insisted that I provide him with medical treatment. Maybe now you have learned a valuable lesson in the way we conduct our war."

Ernie held on to the windshield of the Jeep and fought the urge to be sick.

The losses sustained by the Gunslingers during their assault on Widow's Peak were so high that all the pilots were put on a two-week stand-down. Mike, not wanting to spend two weeks without activity, agreed to fly "slicks," as the UH-1Ds were called, until the Gunslingers were ready for action again.

The slicks had door guns, but nothing else. Albritton, who was Mike's regular door gunner, went with him. Smitty, the crew chief who doubled as the other door gunner, stayed back to work on their aircraft.

After flying Gunslinger missions, the insertion seemed pretty tame, and Albritton was every bit as bored with the routine transportation flight as Mike Carmack.

Occasionally, Albritton would fire off a round at

a water buffalo, but he couldn't coax Mike to fly low enough for him to shoot monkeys. Albritton yawned, blinked his expressionless eyes as they landed to insert a squad of Vietnamese infantry. Albritton looped his mike cord around the neck of the last Vietnamese soldier who disembarked.

Mike took off just as Albritton hooked the Vietnamese soldier, who quickly found himself dangling by his neck some fifty feet above the trees. A soft croaking sound came from his lips and his American M-16 fell from his flailing hands.

"Mr. Carmack," Albritton said laconically, "we've got a gook hooked up."

"What the . . . ?" Mike called out. He racked the helicopter into a tight turn and headed back for the landing area. The small soldier was swinging freely.

Suddenly a stream of 40-mm anti-aircraft fire slashed up from the jungle floor, tore the legs off the Vietnamese soldier, and laced into the bottom of the ship. One final look of surprise showed in the brown eyes, then the soldier was cut loose by the shells and dropped to the jungle floor. Rounds slammed into the fuel tank and transmission deck. The fuel tank exploded in a mass of yellow flames that changed into a stream of fire trailing the aircraft.

Mike fought for control of the helicopter, but it was impossible because the transmission mounts had been knocked loose and excessive vibration had begun. He attempted to set down in the open clearing, but his rpm deteriorated and he had to slip in between two trees, wiping the blades off and banging into the ground. They skidded across the earth, spewing parts and fire.

The nose section ripped free and Mike and Dobbins found themselves dangling unhurt from their seats. They watched the rest of the aircraft smash into a dike and cartwheel several times, finally coming to rest as an inverted burning hulk.

The crew chief, who had jumped out when the aircraft first hit the ground, ran over to them. "Are you two all right, sir?" he yelled, helping them from their seats.

"Yes," Mike replied. "Did both of you get out?"

"Albritton is still in there," the crew chief answered.

Mike started toward what was left of the aircraft, but another explosion drove him back.

The three men stood by, helpless, as the aircraft burned with an angry roar. The horror of the moment was so engrossing that they didn't hear the Huey coming back to pick them up until it was already on the ground.

"Albritton, you dumb shit," Mike said. "Why did you do that? Why did you do that?"

"Come on, Mike," Dobbins called as he started toward the helicopter that had landed for them. "Let's get out of here."

"I can't just leave him," Mike said, pointing to the burning chopper.

"Sure you can," Dobbins called. "Come on, goddammit! There's nothing you can do for him now. Let's get the hell out while we still can!"

Reluctantly, Mike moved over to the rescue

chopper. He had just slipped inside when the pilot picked it up, and the motion of the takeoff rolled him back against the transmission tunnel. Dobbins, who was already strapped down, helped Mike onto the red bench. They circled around once and Mike looked out the door, beyond the tip of the spinning blade, to see the burning remains of what had been his helicopter. He leaned his head back and closed his eyes, fighting the nausea that welled up inside.

The co-pilot turned around and looked toward the back. None of Mike's crew was wearing headsets, so he had to yell his question.

"You guys all right?"

"Yeah," Mike said.

"Jeez! What the hell happened? What'd you go back for?"

"We had a ARVN soldier hung up," Mike said, without telling why he was hung up.

"A damned dink? You went back for a dink? I would've let the son of a bitch fall," the co-pilot said. He turned back around and Mike could see his lips move as he told the pilot what happened. The pilot shook his head.

Mike thought of the weekend just past. He had spent it with Le. It had been a moment of tranquility. Now that moment was gone, the memory slipping away into eternity. Would he ever know such a peaceful moment again?

# Chapter Eleven

The village of Hoa Ginh was proud of the Xa Hoa Pagoda. The pagoda was not only their church, it was their social center as well. It was the largest and most beautiful Buddhist temple in the entire province.

In the Xa Hoa Pagoda in Hoa Ginh, the village faithful had gathered to burn their joss sticks and to make their offerings to Buddha. The air hung heavy with the sweet smell of incense, and the sound of prayer chants echoed melodiously through the cavernous red-and-gold temple.

No one paid any attention to the convoy of vehicles when it rolled through the street of the village, because the army frequently conducted maneuvers in the area. The lead Jeep had a two-way radio and messages coming over it were so loud that they wafted across the landscaped garden of the pagoda like voices from a loudspeaker. But even that didn't cause undue disturbance among the villagers.

The convoy stopped, and South Vietnamese Special Forces poured out of the trucks. Officers shouted commands and gave orders, and the men formed into precise military platoons. This was unusual, so the people stopped and began to watch them.

Colonel Mot had been in the lead Jeep, and he walked along the line of vehicles until he stood in the middle, where he remained to watch the junior officers getting the soldiers into formation. A little girl stepped up to him and jerked his pant leg. When Mot looked down she held her hand out, palm up, already an expert in the art of begging. Mot ignored her.

"Colonel, the detail is formed," one of the officers reported. Mot returned the officer's salute, then raised his arm to look at his watch. For several moments there was an eerie tableau vivant, illuminated by the brightness of the moon. Colonel Mot stood silently, his arm crooked, staring at his watch. The soldiers were in neat lines, absolutely motionless, faces devoid of all expression.

The villagers appeared mesmerized by the scene, neither moving nor talking. The prayer chants and cymbals had stilled, and the village was in absolute quiet. The only sound was the flat clanking of a cowbell. It was hanging from the neck of a water buffalo that was tethered and grazing nearby. Occasionally a rush of static would pop over the two-way radio in the command Jeep.

"Commence the operation," Mot said quietly.

What happened next was totally unexpected, and everyone stood rooted in shock, unable to react until it was too late. One of the officers shouted a command, and the neat military ranks surged forward, yelling and brandishing truncheons, attacking everyone.

The screams of fear and pain were drowned out by the sound of destruction as the buildings were set ablaze and the meager furnishings smashed.

In house after house the hiding places of the most prized possessions were discovered, and the treasures — perhaps a flashlight, a packet of steel needles, or an oil lantern — were destroyed or stolen by the soldiers. The women begged and cried, and the men shouted in anger. But they were clubbed into silence.

Gradually all the villagers were herded toward the pagoda and forced inside, shaking in terror and rage.

For several seconds there was no further activity on the part of the soldiers. Everything was silent save the continuous clanking of the cowbell as the buffalo quietly grazed, oblivious of the destruction going on around him.

Colonel Mot took a battery-powered loudspeaker and spoke to the people inside the pagoda.

"Attention! Attention! As commander of this area, I have declared a state of martial law. One of the restrictions of the law is the Pagoda Assembly

Act. All buildings of the Buddhist religion are to be used for religious purposes only. The gathering in such a building of anyone for any purpose other than religion is strictly prohibited. I order that the Xa Hoa Pagoda be evacuated immediately.''

Mot put the loudspeaker down, and a handful of terrorized citizens started to leave the pagoda. A squad of soldiers rushed at them and began beating them, forcing them back inside. Mot watched the proceedings impassively.

"You have only thirty seconds remaining in which to evacuate," Mot said over the loudspeaker again. "I plead with you to do so at once!"

A few others tried to leave, but they, too, were driven back inside by the soldiers.

"You were warned, and your time has expired," Mot said.

Inside the pagoda the people were wild with terror. They knew now that the soldiers wouldn't let them leave. They also knew they were all about to die.

"Look!" one of them shouted. He pointed to a hissing object that had been tossed in by one of the soldiers. That object was soon joined by several others, and then, with a popping sound, tear gas began spewing thickly, nauseatingly, from the small gray canisters.

The terror turned to hysteria, and the wheezing, crying mob surged for the doors. Many were cut down by rifle fire, others by skull-smashing blows, as the troops quieted them with grim efficiency. Fires licked at the night sky. Silhouetted against the orange flames, soldiers could be seen dumping buckets of feces from the community toilets into the community wells.

"Recall the detail," Colonel Mot ordered.

Shouted commands from the officers brought the troops back to the trucks, where they climbed on board as calmly as if boarding a bus. Mot pulled out a silk handkerchief and looked over the destroyed village as he wiped his hands. He climbed back into the lead Jeep and signaled for the convoy to leave.

When the convoy pulled out they would leave behind a burned-out village. The screaming, shouting, and rattle of musketry had stilled. Now there was only the crying of a child and the crackling of the flames. The stunned survivors stared at their destroyed village in disbelief as the trucks roared away.

Colonel Mot led the convoy down Highway 13 to their next stop, Di An. Di An was much larger than Hoa Ginh, so he wouldn't be able to sack and pillage the whole town. However, he planned to destroy the pagoda and to bring back the patriarch of the Buddhist sect there, a priest named Vu Dinh Duc. Though he had no proof, Mot believed that Vu Dinh Duc was a V.C. officer.

The pagoda was on a square in the middle of the town, and as it burned, it created a glowing circle of light in the black of the night. Just beyond the wavering flames the people of the town gathered in a large crowd and stood in the protective cloak of darkness. They watched in fearful silence as Mot's soldiers methodically destroyed the relics of the pagoda, some of which were more than a thousand years old. Colonel Mot kept glancing cautiously toward the crowd, alert for any possible uprising, but no one showed any sign of resisting.

"Colonel Mot, we cannot find Vu Dinh Duc," one of the officers reported.

"Question some of the villagers," Mot ordered.

"We have captured three who were attempting to hide a relic. I questioned them, but they would say nothing."

"Bring them to me."

Mot had been leaning against his Jeep watching both the work of his men and the actions of the crowd that had gathered in the darkness. He walked to the center of the square and stood there, his feet spread apart, his hands on his hips. He looked at the fire and watched a piece of fire-blackened paper tumble crazily as it rode a column of heat and smoke high into the night sky.

"Here are the three," the young lieutenant said, pushing three sullen men in front of him.

Mot looked at them for a moment. Their hands had been tied behind their backs. There were marks on their faces from where they had been beaten.

"Do you know where Vu Dinh Duc is?" Mot asked calmly.

"Yes, but we will not turn him over to dogs," the one in the middle said.

Mot looked at the one who had spoken. He was taller than Mot. His features, combined with the look of pride and determination on his face, were a classic representation of the ideal Vietnamese folk hero. The man was young and handsome, and his strength and virility moved Mot to an almost sexual ecstasy. Mot reached up and touched the young man's face, letting his fingers caress his smooth features.

"You will not tell us?" Mot asked, and his question was delivered in a silken, almost apologetic tone of voice.

"No!" the young man spat. "Never!"

Mot pulled his pistol from his holster and pointed it at the man. He pulled the trigger without saying another word, as the pop of the .45 echoed through the square. The young man pitched backward and fell down dead.

"Will you tell us?" Mot asked the second of the two prisoners. His voice was agonizingly calm.

The second man looked at his dead comrade, and then at Mot. His body began to jerk convulsively and his lips trembled, but he said nothing.

Mot shot him, then turned his gun on the last of the three.

"I will tell! I will tell!" the third one began yelling. He cried and begged that his life be spared, sinking to his knees in supplication.

Mot put his pistol back in the holster and looked at the lieutenant. "I don't believe you'll have any trouble now," he said with an evil grin.

"Thank you, Colonel," the lieutenant said, grabbing his prisoner roughly.

Colonel Mot wiped his hands with his silk handkerchief again, then returned to his Jeep to watch. A few moments later a group of Mot's men returned, laughing and yelling obscenities at an old man. They had a rope tied around his neck. The man was around eighty-five, hollow-cheeked and extraordinarily frail. His skin had the texture of parchment, and the hair of his beard was as fine as threads of silk. His eyes were downcast, but he was not frightened as he stood before Mot.

"Throw him in the truck," Mot ordered.

Vu Dinh Duc was dragged to the last truck in the convoy and thrown on board. Then, his night's work finished, Mot ordered the convoy back to Saigon.

When Mot returned to his villa, he went straight to his wife's room, then kicked open the door and turned on the light. Le, suddenly awakened by the noise and the harsh white glare, sat up quickly, pulling a silk sheet to her chin. She didn't normally share a room with her husband, and his entry at any time was a rare occurrence. At this hour it was unheard of.

Mot looked at Le, and the expression on his face frightened her. He held his hands out to her. "I have blood on these hands," he said excitedly.

Le looked at his hands in confusion. They were clean. "What are you talking about?" she asked. "There is no blood."

"Smell them," Mot ordered. He sat on the edge of the bed and thrust his hands beneath Le's nose.

Le noticed nothing about his hands, but his clothes smelled of smoke.

"What a grand night this has been!" Mot said, his eyes looking just over Le's head, as if he were seeing something in the distance.

Mot turned the palms of his hands up and looked at them. "There was one . . . a young man. He was beautiful, such well-formed features. And . . . can you understand? I wanted him . . . sexually . . . but not homosexually. I can't put it into words, but when I killed him I felt as if I had just had a woman. I didn't come, but the sensation was there as if I had."

Le had never seen Mot like this. It was terrifying. She moved across the bed to get away from him. "What are you talking about?" As Le moved, the sheet dropped down to expose one of her breasts. Mot, seeing this, grabbed the sheet and jerked it back so that Le was totally exposed. He smiled at her.

"Be the young man for me," he said.

"What?"

"The young man I killed. I told you, I wanted him sexually. You can take his place for me."

"No," she said.

"You can't deny me," Mot replied. "I'm your husband. You can't deny me. Pretend I am your American, as I am pretending you are the young man."

Mot undressed quickly, then grabbed Le and pulled her across the bed to him, mashing his mouth roughly against hers. He squeezed her breasts savagely, raking his hands across her chest, leaving a trail of scratches.

At first Le tried to resist him, but then she correctly reasoned that that was exactly what Mot wanted. So she remained as passive as possible. When Mot forced her down on the bed, she obligingly spread her legs so that his entry would not be brutal.

Mot was lost in his own drive for fulfillment. He was not aware of Le's reaction. He was insatiable. The only sounds in the room were the slapping of flesh against flesh and Mot's animal-like moans.

He jerked and thrust against her with a savage fury, finally collapsing across her.

Le stayed beneath him for several moments, fearful that any movement on her part would activate him again. Finally the raspy breathing in her ear achieved a steady rhythm and she slid out from under him. She looked down at him in total revulsion. He was on his stomach, his mouth was open, and a small string of spittle trickled onto the bed.

Le took a bath, making the water much hotter than she normally would, trying to scald away the unclean feeling. When she was finished she went upstairs to one of the guest rooms. She locked herself inside, then collapsed across the bed and cried until just before dawn, when she fell asleep from exhaustion.

# Chapter Twelve

In his apartment over on Le Loi, Ernie was waking up at about the same time Le was falling asleep. It was still dark outside. It was too early even for the dawn people. Ernie would normally have been asleep, but the section of Saigon in which he lived was experiencing one of the frequent electrical failures, and the fans had stopped.

The heat began collecting in Ernie's bedroom, enveloping him in its oppressive weight and bathing him in perspiration. With no breeze to keep them away, the mosquitoes began buzzing around him. They were so tiny that they could land, take several bites, then fly away before Ernie was aware of them. Their bites couldn't be felt, but the anticoagulant toxin they injected was powerful,

139

and the irritation and itching of ten to twenty bites was maddening.

Ernie awoke with his nerves raw from the itching. He sought some relief by taking a shower. Then he took a bath in mosquito repellent, using two whole bottles. The repellent had an unpleasant odor and burned his skin, but it kept the mosquitoes off.

Ernie tried to go back to bed, but there wasn't a breath of air moving in his room. After a few minutes he walked out onto the balcony of his third-floor apartment.

There was a slight breeze. Ernie opened a Coke and sat on his balcony naked, taking advantage of what little air there was outside.

By the time he had finished his Coke the city began waking up, and the morning people had begun their rounds. Ernie watched the birth of the new day. Before the sun rose in Vietnam the eastern sky was spread with a great palette of color, starting with purple and dark blue, then turning to red, orange, yellow, and finally the silver of day as the sun disk became completely visible.

Ernie looked down on the street and watched an old woman set up her portable sidewalk café on the corner of Le Loi and Tu Do. Le Loi, Tu Do, Duong Truoung Tan Buu, Cong Ly, Tru Minh Ky, Thru Ming Gaing — the streets of Saigon were as intimately known to Ernie as the streets of his hometown. In fact, Ernie chuckled to himself, Saigon was now more of a hometown than Jackson, Mississippi. The streets of Jackson — Bailey Avenue, Fortification, Poindexter, Capitol — were only names to him now. Try as he might, he could no longer match vivid images with the individual streets. Ernie left the balcony and dressed for work.

"Did you hear?" Ernie was asked when he reported for work. "The Black Knight broke up the V.C. infrastructure last night. There's going to be a major operation today that could break the back of the V.C. forever."

"That's a pretty bold statement," Ernie said. "Break their back forever?"

"It's a joint operation between the ARVN Special Forces and the American forces at Phu Loi."

"At Phu Loi? Will the Gunslingers be a part of it?"

"I imagine they will, yes. Why? You going to go see your friend?"

"Soon as I can find a way up there," Ernie replied.

"I thought you might. That's why I saved you a seat on the press chopper. You better hurry, he's taking off in about twenty minutes."

"Gentlemen, the commanding officer," the adjutant announced, and all the officers who had gathered in the mess stood as Todaro entered the room.

Mike looked around at the other Gunslingers. Dobbins was a familiar face, so was Wilson and a couple of others, but there were lots of what the E.M. called F.N.G.s — fuckin' new guys — mixed in with them, assigned to replace those who had been lost during the attack on Widow's Peak.

Many had yet to fly a combat mission, and even the ones Mike called the greenest of the green were being paired with the F.N.G.s to provide some level of experience in every ship.

No longer would Mike have the luxury of flying with Dobbins. Dobbins, though still a W-1, had been in-country for six months and was given his own crew. Mike had to break in a new co-pilot and door gunner. Only Smitty was still with him.

"Gentlemen," Todaro said, "please be seated." Chairs scraped as the officers sat again. Most had coffee and cigarettes, and they began drinking as they listened to the briefing.

"This is big, fellas, real big," Todaro said. "Last night, Colonel Mot conducted raids against the very heart of the V.C. These are the people who give the orders and furnish the support for Charley. I've been told on very good authority that the raid was extremely successful . . . Now we've got a couple thousand V.C. running around out in the jungle like chickens with their heads cut off. They have no one to lead them, no idea of where to go. We can move in, mop them up, and wipe out the entire nest in one operation. After that the only way the North Vietnamese can continue the war is to bring down their army . . . and, gentlemen, that they are afraid to do. Why, we could end the war with this one operation."

"Who are we transporting, Colonel? Americans or ARVNs?"

"The transport assignments have been carefully worked out. The Americans are being taken in by their own lift companies. That means we'll take in the ARVN Special Forces. Gunslingers?''

"Yes, sir," Captain Wilson answered.

"You'll operate in fire teams of four helicopters per team. Team designations: Red, White, and Blue. Put your most experienced men, regardless of rank, in command of the fire teams."

"Yes, sir," Wilson replied.

"I'd like to see you and Mr. Carmack as soon as the briefing concludes."

"Yes, sir."

Mike looked over at Mr. Morris, his co-pilot. Morris, a brand-new W-1, had just graduated from flight school and arrived in-country two days ago. He looked like a kid who got on the wrong school bus one morning and wound up in Nam, instead of Central High.

"Take care of the pre-flight for me, will you, Walt?"

"Yes, sir!" Morris answered eagerly.

Mike winced. "You really don't have to call me 'sir,' " he said. "Some second lieutenant might hear that and the next thing you know he'll be wanting me to say 'sir' to him."

"Okay," Walt said. "Oh . . . uh . . . Mr. Carmack, everyone says I'm lucky to be flying with you."

"Yeah? Did you ask Albritton?"

"Who?"

"Never mind. Just take care of the pre-flight."

"I'll get right on it," Morris said, hurrying out of the room.

"God," Mike said to Captain Wilson. "I was never . . . never . . . never that eager."

Wilson chuckled. "I think you were born with a thousand hours," he said. "Come on, let's see what Todaro wants."

"Well, Captain Wilson, Mr. Carmack," Todaro said a few moments later. "What do you think about the new guys? You think they're up to it?"

"It's not the new guys I'm worried about," Mike said.

"Well, what are you worried about?"

"The pilots we have with the new guys," Mike said. "Colonel, do you realize that some of our 'experienced' pilots have no more than two or three missions under their belts? And they're flying as plane commanders. It's a case of the blind leading the blind."

"Perhaps so," Colonel Todaro replied. "But there's really nothing we can do about it now, is there?"

"No, sir, I guess not," Mike said.

"At least we don't have the guns at Widow's Peak to worry about," Colonel Todaro said.

"Why not?"

"Part of the operational orders," Colonel Todaro said. "I asked the air force to take them out with napalm."

"Colonel, why the hell didn't you let them do it in the first place?" Mike asked.

"I'll not be second-guessed by a goddamned warrant officer!" Colonel Todaro spat. "I did what I thought was right. That's all anyone can do."

"Yeah, well, I'd better get out to the flight line," Mike said.

"Mike?" Colonel Todaro called, and there was a plaintive quality to his voice, the tone of one who was asking for forgiveness, if not understanding.

"Yes, sir?"

"Uh . . . good luck," Colonel Todaro said.

"Thanks," Mike answered.

Ernie stood out on the flight line watching the activity around the helicopters. Ships were being pre-flighted, guns were being loaded, gear was being thrown aboard. He saw Mike's helicopter, but didn't recognize the gunner or the young warrant officer who was standing on the transmission deck looking at the rotor head. He started to look somewhere else when he saw Smitty.

"Smitty," he called. "How are you?"

"Hey, Mr. Chapel, how's it hangin'?" Smitty called.

"What's all this?" Ernie asked, taking in the new gunner and young warrant officer.

"Me 'n' Mr. Carmack are the only ones left from the old crew," Smitty said.

"Where's Dobbins? Albritton?"

"You didn't hear about Albritton?"

"No."

"He's a crispy critter," Smitty said.

Ernie winced. A "crispy critter" was the macabre term the men used for describing someone who had been killed in a fire.

"I'm sorry," Ernie said. "I hadn't heard."

"It happened last week," Smitty said. "Five-oh-one was still on red-X from the Widow's Peak mission. I was here workin' on the ship, but Albritton, Mr. Carmack, and Mr. Dobbins took a slick to off-load some slopes. One of them got hung up as he was jumpin' down, and Mr. Carmack, he turned back to let him down when they run right into ground fire. The slick was shot down and Albritton and the dink were killed. No one else was hurt."

"I'm sorry to hear about Albritton," Ernie said. "But I'm glad everyone else got out."

"Yeah, it's hard enough breakin' in a new co-pilot and gunner. I'd hate to have to break in a whole new crew. Oh, here comes Mr. Carmack."

Ernie walked out to greet Mike, who smiled and returned his greeting.

"I hear you're going to end the war today," Ernie said.

"That's the poop from group," Mike said. "You want to go along?"

"You don't mind?"

Mike looked at the new door gunner and co-pilot, then laughed. "Hell, no, I'd welcome the experience," he said. "Get a brain bucket and get on board."

"Mr. Carmack, the transponder's out," Morris said.

Mike looked at Smitty. "What happened to the transponder?"

"Avionics took it when we were down," Smitty said. "They never replaced it."

"I want it back. If you have to make a midnight requisition, I want it back."

"Yes, sir," Smitty said, smiling broadly. "I was kinda hopin' you'd feel that way."

"Thanks for letting me go," Ernie said.

"Yeah, well, I can't promise you any action today," Mike said. "Captain Wilson just told me he wants me to keep my fire team on standby. We'll just orbit the area and observe, unless we're specifically needed."

"You won't get any complaints from me," Ernie said. "This way I'll have a good ringside seat for the action without having to get involved."

Half an hour later Mike and the three other helicopters of Blue team were orbiting over the area of operations with little probability of getting involved. Gunships from Gunslinger had raced back and forth pouring fire into the treelines around the little village, but no one was reporting any return fire. When the slicks landed and the troops jumped off, not one round was reported. If they really were in the middle of a couple of thousand V.C., the V.C. were strangely quiet.

Twenty miles away, stretched out along Route 15, was an American supply convoy of ten trucks.

"Keep your eyes open, Simmons," the captain in charge of the convoy told his driver. The captain held an M-16 on his lap and patted it nervously.

"Cap'n Mack, if I open my lids any wider, my eyeballs are goin' to fall out," Simmons said. Simmons was SP-5 Edward Simmons, a red-haired boy from Wyoming. "I reckon my ancestors felt like this when they was lookin' for Indians," he said.

"Vexation Six, this is Three, over," the Jeep radio popped. Vexation Three was Lieutenant Appleby, riding in the last vehicle, a trail Jeep.

Mack reached for the mike.

"This is Six, go ahead."

"I just caught sight of someone on the hill behind us. I think we are about to have company."

"Do you mean ambush?" Mack asked anxiously.

"Could be."

The last two words were no sooner out of Appleby's mouth than there was an explosion in the road just ahead of them. It was so close that dirt and rock rained down on them.

"Jesus!" Simmons shouted. "Oh, sweet Jesus! They're comin' after us!"

There were several other explosions along the line behind them and Mack twisted around in his seat to see one of the trucks burning. The V.C. had planted charges in the road along the killing zone. Then they set off the charges when the convoy was in place. Fortunately, the spacing of the vehicles in the convoy was such that only one truck was hit by the planted charges.

There was no way to drive out of the ambush, so Simmons stopped, then climbed into the machine gun ring in the back seat. He pointed the machine gun, a heavy .50-caliber, toward the hillside and began firing. Captain Mack got on the radio.

"What's the air force push?" Mack yelled.

"It's pre-set by channels," Simmons answered. "One for air force, two for navy, three for army."

Mack turned to channel one.

"Hello, any air, any air, this is Vexation. Come in, please."

A bullet careened off the machine gun ring and pieces of it shaved off, hitting Mack in the face, stinging in a dozen different spots.

"Any air, any air, come in," he called again.

Not getting an answer from the air force, he tried the navy, and when that one drew a blank he switched to army.

"Any air, any air, this is Vexation, come in."

Mike heard the call and he changed his transmitter to match the receiver. "Vexation, this is Gunslinger."

"Gunslinger, what are you? Do you have ordinance?"

"That's affirmative, I have four hogs."

"I need ground support, Gunslinger. I've been ambushed and I'm being chewed to pieces."

"Who are you, Vexation?" Mike asked.

"I'm a supply convoy with the 765th Battalion. I need help, bad!"

"Roger, Vexation. Where are you?"

"About ten clicks west of Binh Loc on Route 15. Right after you cross the river."

"Near the stone quarry?"

"Yes, about a click west of the stone quarry. How soon can you get here?"

"About ten minutes," Mike said. "Can you hold on that long?"

"I don't have any choice," Mack answered. "Get here fast as you can."

"We're on our way."

"I'll pop smoke," Mack said. "But you can't miss us, we're the ones gettin' our ass shot off."

Mike flipped channels. "Blue team, this is Six. We have a fire mission. Follow me out."

"All right, this is more like it!" one of the young warrants said.

Mike flipped channels again, then called Colonel Todaro.

"Gunslinger Six, this is Blue Six. Request permission to answer a call for ground support."

"Negative, Blue Six," Todaro replied, and Mike could hear the irritation in his voice.

"It's a supply convoy, Gunslinger Six. He's in trouble."

"He can get air force support."

"Maybe, but he called me. If I don't get there in a couple of minutes it'll be too late."

"Wait one, Blue Six. Let me confirm," Todaro said.

"Okay," Mike said, without broadcasting. "I'll wait for confirmation, but while I'm waiting, I'm going to Binh Loc."

About seven minutes later he still had no answer, but he saw the convoy with a couple of burning trucks. He also saw several black-clad soldiers inching down the hill toward the convoy.

"I see you, Gunslinger, I'm popping smoke," Vexation said.

"Roger, confirm yellow smoke," Mike said.

"Blue Six, this is Gunslinger Six."

"Go ahead, Gunslinger Six."

"Negative on the support. I checked with MACV and the air force is on its way. They should be there in one-zero minutes.

"I'm here now, and if I don't respond, there won't be anyone left for the air force to save."

"Return to your station at once, Blue Six."

Mike flipped off the selector switch. "Smitty, when they took the transponder they screwed up the radios. I couldn't hear what the colonel said, could you?"

"Didn't hear anything," Smitty said. "Come on, Mr. Carmack, let's kill some dinks."

"Blue flight, your target is on the hill approaching the convoy," Mike said. "Let's go."

Mike made a pass over the road, firing rockets and machine guns. There was another hog right beside him, and between the two of them the entire hillside was under fire. He pulled up at the end of his run, loading the rotor disc so that Ernie could feel the G-force of the turn. He twisted around in his seat and looked behind him to see the other two make their pass.

"Pretty good job, guys!" Vexation called. "You stopped them cold."

"Here we come again," Mike said, dropping the pitch and rolling the cyclic forward to start his second strafing run. Now he could see dozens of bodies lying in the paddy, and the formation, which had been advancing so confidently against the handful of marines, was starting back toward the wood line on the opposite side of the field.

"Army helicopters, are you on this push?"

"Roger. Who's calling?" Mike answered.

"You got your basic air force reaction team here, two Phantoms with enough napalm to barbecue Omaha. If you'll just scoot out of the way and let the big boys go to work, we'll take care of this little business for you."

"Thanks, air force," Vexation said. "But you ought to know that if the Gunslingers hadn't showed up, we wouldn't need your napalm."

"Gunslingers, huh? Like Wyatt Earp?"

The air force pilot was talking as calmly as if he

were sitting behind a desk, yet all the while his plane was climbing away from the first attack with a sheet of fire spreading behind and below.

"Sort of like that," Mike said. He looked at the destruction caused by the napalm and whistled. "It's all yours, guys. Have fun."

"Tell you what, Gunslinger. Those damned whirlybirds fly too long in the same place. When folks are shooting at me, I like to haul ass."

"That's what I'm doing now," Mike said. "I'm doing a hundred knots."

"God, such speed," the air force pilot said sarcastically. "It takes my breath away. Well, there you go, Vexation, just turn them once and they'll be done. Hold on, Gunslinger, we're coming by."

Both jets zoomed by, rocking their wings in salute as they passed, flying so fast that Mike and the others bounced in their wake. Behind them the entire hill was burning and the ambush on the convoy was completely broken up.

# Chapter Thirteen

Mike flipped the selector switch back to Todaro's frequency.

"Gunslinger Six, this is Blue Six, re-establishing contact. Over."

"Blue Six, report to me as soon as you land," Todaro said angrily.

"Roger, Gunslinger Six."

"What's going to happen to us?" Morris asked.

Mike looked over at Morris and smiled. "Nothing's going to happen to you. You had to go where I took you. I'm the one with his ass in the crack."

"Mr. Carmack, want me to fuck up the radio?" Smitty asked.

"Don't worry about it," Mike said. "There's not a hell of a lot he can do when you get right down to it. Let's get back to the operational area and see what's happening. From the way things were going this morning, it was a complete bust. That's probably why Todaro is so pissed off.''

It was about a ten-minute flight back to the operational area, and during that ten minutes Mike wondered what Todaro would say. If there had been no firefight on the operation, there wasn't much Todaro would say. He would have to balance a disobeyed order against the rescue of the supply convoy, and Mike was pretty sure that Vexation, whoever he was, would come to his defense if it ever came to that. The truth was, it would never come to that. Todaro would make an ass of himself if he tried to press it.

"Hey, Mr. Carmack, what the hell's goin' on down there?" Smitty suddenly called.

"Where? What are you talking about?"

"Look down there, between those hootches and the river! What's happening down there?"

Mike looked where Smitty indicated, and he saw it, too. A group of villagers — men, women, and children — stood huddled together while a line of black-clad soldiers was standing off to one side. There was a winking of muzzle flashes from the black-clad soldiers. Then the villagers began falling to the ground.

"What the hell! That's V.C.!" Morris shouted. "Look, Mr. Carmack. They're executing the villagers!"

"Gunslinger Six, we've got V.C. on the ground over here at the village on the river," Mike said.

"Negative, that area is cleared," Gunslinger Six replied.

"Jesus! Mr. Carmack, they just shot another bunch. They're executin' the whole damned village!" Smitty said.

Mike reached for the transponder, then drew his hand back. "Shit, no parrot! There's no way we can identify them."

"There goes another bunch, sir!" Smitty called.

"Dobbins! You got a parrot?"

"Roger."

"Squawk."

"No response, Mike."

"All right, let's hit them," Mike said. "Be careful of the villagers."

Mike whipped the Huey around in a tight turn, dropped pitch, and rolled forward, coming down like a dive bomber. Morris opened up on them, and as they passed by, the two door guns joined the shooting.

After Mike's run, two more Hueys made a pass at the soldiers, and within minutes several of their bodies littered the ground, along with the bodies of the villagers who had been executed.

"Blue Six, Blue Six, cease fire, cease fire! They are friendlies, they are friendlies!" Dobbins said. "I picked them up on Fox Mike and they squawked my parrot!"

"My God," Mike said, feeling sick.

"I've got a follow-up," Dobbins said. "We've just killed two American advisors, fourteen ARVN troops, and Colonel Mot."

# Chapter Fourteen

Ernie rolled the paper out of the typewriter and read it. He had filed several thousand words since this war started, but so far this was the story he least wanted to write.

In every war there have been court-martials. There have even been court-martials for murder . . . but as far as this reporter has been able to learn, there has never been a murder trial quite like the one coming up in Saigon.

Michael Timothy Carmack, Chief Warrant Officer, Grade 3, is a helicopter pilot. He is a very good helicopter pilot and has been decorated for bravery many times over.

Two weeks ago, Mr. Carmack led a helicopter attack team that strafed and killed fourteen South

Vietnamese soldiers, two American advisors, and Colonel Ngyuet Cao Mot. Mr. Carmack claims, and with some justification, that it was a case of mistaken identity. In fact, this reporter was on board Mr. Carmack's helicopter during the actual event, and I can attest that the ARVN soldiers were wearing black, a color associated with V.C.

The U.S. Army's charges against Mr. Carmack are based on the fact that, against specific orders to the contrary, Mr. Carmack left his assigned station during the operation, then returned and, again against specific orders, led the attack against what he thought were V.C. troops.

That friendly soldiers were killed is tragic, and that Mr. Carmack disobeyed orders is an offense triable by court-martial, but those two things together do not constitute a charge of murder. The charge of murder stems from the fact that Colonel Mot was killed by a man who, it is alleged, was Madam Mot's lover. According to the South Vietnamese Defense Ministry, who asked that the U.S. Army bring the charges, Mr. Carmack used the cover of mistaken identity to kill Colonel Mot so that Madam Mot would be free.

This allegation of sexual intimacy has been backed up, reportedly by a young house-girl employee of the Mot villa who claims to have actually seen Mr. Carmack and Madam Mot having intercourse. Though the house girl is only twelve years old, her testimony is very damaging.

If Mr. Carmack is found guilty of first-degree murder, he could, under military law, be executed by firing squad.

"Murder?" Le asked Colonel Phat. Colonel Phat was the survivor's assistance officer assigned to her after her husband had been killed. "You mean to tell me that Mike Carmack is being tried for murder?"

"Yes," Phat said.

"Why? Why would they do such a thing?"

"Because they have reason to believe that it was murder."

"Why would Mr. Carmack murder my husband?"

Phat stared at the floor in embarrassment. "It's . . . it's not for me to comment on some things," he said.

Le gasped and put her hand to her mouth. "My God! Because he was my lover? They think he killed my husband because he was my lover?"

"Yes."

"But, that's not true! What would he have to gain? My husband knew of my affairs. Mr. Carmack knew that he knew. There would be no advantage in killing Mot."

"Perhaps the American thought that, without a husband, you would be free to marry him," Phat suggested.

Le laughed. "Believe me, Colonel Phat, marriage was the most distant thing from my mind . . . or Mr. Carmack's. Maybe we can get this stopped. Maybe I can talk to someone."

"Who?"

"Someone in the defense ministry. Perhaps if I go to them, plead with them, they can pressure the Americans not to go through with this trial."

"Madam Mot, you would be better off if you stayed out of this completely," Colonel Phat said.

"Stay out of it? I certainly will not stay out of it.

Not if there is the chance that Mr. Carmack will be found guilty for something he didn't do. I want to talk to someone in the defense ministry.''

"You don't understand," Phat said. "It was our defense ministry who persuaded the Americans to bring the charge of murder.''

"Why?"

"There are other forces in play here, Madam Mot. Political forces," Colonel Phat said.

"I don't care what other forces are in play. I want to go to the defense ministry and get this stopped.''

"Very well," Phat said with a sigh. "Let me go first. I'll find someone for you to talk to. You stay here until I get back.''

"Why can't I go with you?"

"It would be better if you stayed here.''

"All right. But let me know what you found out as soon as you get back.''

Le waited patiently for several hours, then was convinced that Colonel Phat had no intention of returning. She decided she would go by herself. She called her driver.

"I can't take you," the driver said.

"What do you mean, you can't take me?"

"Colonel Phat said you weren't to leave the house unless he authorized it.''

"Unless he authorized it? Look here, do you mean to tell me I am a prisoner in my own home?''

"No, madam.''

"But I can't leave?"

"No, madam.''

Le turned and walked back into her house. She stood just inside the door for a few minutes, thinking. A moment later, wearing a black *ao dai*, she sneaked through the back door, through the back gate, and out onto the street. A cyclo came by and she hailed it, then asked to be taken to the defense ministry.

It was dusk, and the clouds that had hung over the city all day made it even darker. It wasn't actually raining, but there was a slight mist, and as she was riding in the open seat of the motorcycle, it blew against her face with a stinging spray.

They drove by a row of bars that catered primarily to Americans. There were scores of prostitutes in front of the bars, all wearing brightly colored Western-style dresses, heavy makeup, and false eyelashes. They were throwing their arms around the American soldiers and propositioning them openly. The soldiers were laughing and pinching them, or kissing and fondling the women's breasts. For one insane moment, Le thought about having the cyclo driver stop. She wished she could go into one of the bars and begin working the soldiers, right alongside the other girls. She wished she could just lose herself in the anonymity of what the American soldiers called "Plantation Row."

Ten minutes later she paid her cyclo driver and stood in the blue haze of his exhaust smoke as he drove off. She walked up to the gate of the defense ministry where two Vietnamese soldiers were standing guard.

"I am Madam Mot," she said. "I would like to speak with General Linh."

"I know . . . you're Madam Mot, and I'm Emperor Bao Dai."

"No, please, I really am Madam Mot."

"Wait a minute," the other said quickly. He looked at Le for a second. "She's telling the truth. She really is Madam Mot."

"How do you know?"

"I've seen her picture, hundreds of times."

"I'm sorry, madam," the first guard apologized. "I didn't recognize you."

"That's all right. Now, please, may I be taken to see General Linh?"

"Yes, of course. Come inside with me, madam. I'll get an officer to help you."

The guard took Le into the building and told her to wait in one of the anterooms. As luck would have it, he had gone no more than twenty steps down the hall when he saw Colonel Phat.

"Colonel Phat, I have Madam Mot in the anteroom."

"What? What's she doing here?"

"I don't know, sir. She just showed up. I don't know what to do with her. I told her I would find an officer for her."

"All right, thank you, I'll take care of it," Phat said. He went into the anteroom.

"Oh, Colonel Phat, I'm glad you're here. Have you found out anything? Could you please tell me what's going on?"

"Come with me," Colonel Phat said.

Le followed him out into the hall, then down a narrow flight of stairs into the basement. When they reached the basement she looked around in confusion.

"Why did we come down here?"

"So we could talk privately."

"Talk privately? About what?"

"I'm sorry, Madam Mot, but your husband was plotting a coup."

"A coup?"

"Yes. The big operation was just to reposition his forces so that only those men loyal to us would be in position when the time came."

"Loyal to us? You mean you were involved, too?"

"Among others. That's why Mr. Carmack must be charged with murder."

"I don't understand. What has one got to do with the other?"

"Mr. Carmack is what you might call a sacrificial lamb. By charging him with murder, all the attention will be drawn to him . . . and to the rather juicy details of your sex life. I, and those with me, feel that the smoke screen thrown up by such a trial will keep anyone from discovering what Colonel Mot was really up to."

"And you expect me to keep quiet about that?"

"Perhaps for the sake of your husband's memory?" Phat suggested.

"Colonel Phat, I have no intention of letting an innocent man be tried for murder to protect my husband's memory, or you, or any of the gang of traitors you work with," Le said angrily.

"Yes," Phat said with a small, oily voice. "I was rather afraid of that." He sighed, then unbuttoned the flap over his pistol.

# Chapter Fifteen

J. W. "Greyhound" Reynolds was one of the best-known criminal lawyers in America. He had read Ernie's articles about the trial, then called Ernie long distance from Houston to see if Mike Carmack would use him.

"I don't think he can afford you," Ernie told him.

"Hell, mister, I know damned well he can't afford me," Greyhound answered in his booming voice. "Not if he pledged half of everything he earned for the rest of his life and threw in his firstborn son."

"Then why do you want to defend him?"

"Let's just say that every now 'n' again I take a case on its merits, just to keep the wheels of justice oiled up a bit." Greyhound chuckled. "Besides, this case has already generated quite a following. If I win, it's going to be worth all I put in it. You can't buy the publicity I'm going to get when this case is tried."

The Universal Code of Military Justice supplied military lawyers for all accused, but it did make allowances for civilian lawyers, should the defendant desire one. Getting the army's permission for Greyhound Reynolds to take the case was easy. It was a little more difficult to convince Mike.

"Look, Ernie, you were in the helicopter with me. You, of all people, know I didn't do that on purpose. You know I'm innocent. Nothing's going to happen to me. I don't need a high-powered lawyer like Greyhound Reynolds."

"You ever read anything about a man called Dreyfus?" Ernie asked.

"No. Who was he?"

"He was a Jewish officer in the French Army around the turn of the century. He was accused of treason, but he was innocent and he counted on that innocence to save him. What he didn't know was that the French Army was conspiring to find him guilty, and the fact that he was innocent didn't mean a damned thing."

"Are you saying the army is conspiring to find me guilty?"

"Maybe not, but someone is. And Madam Mot's suicide certainly hasn't helped your case any."

"I wonder why she did that?" Mike said. "I don't understand it. Unless it wasn't suicide. Ernie, what if she was murdered?"

"Look," Ernie said, "let's not get involved in another case now, okay? Let's just take care of the one at hand. Now, are you going to let Reynolds defend you or not?"

"All right," Mike finally agreed. "Bring him on."

The court-martial was held at Tan Son Nhut in a large administration building that had been cleared of desks and file cabinets and converted over for the purpose. Inside the building, the sun streamed in through the plexiglass windows and the bright beams picked up a million dust motes floating in the still air of the Quonset hut-type building. The air conditioners hummed and rattled and the one nearest the defense table was dripping water. Mike watched the drops fall into a little puddle, spreading concentric circles, while the court-martial board was sworn in.

After the swearing-in ceremony, Mike looked at the board, and his eyes fell on Colonel Arthur Sherman, the president of the court. Colonel Sherman had a curly mop of brindled hair, large brown eyes, a ruddy complexion, and a neatly trimmed moustache. Mike shifted his gaze from Sherman to the other officers on the board. There were three warrant officers on the board, and all three were aviators. Mike was glad of that. However, none of the commissioned officers was an aviator, and he was disappointed by that.

There was more ceremony, much of it incomprehensible to Mike, until finally the trial counsel, Major Patterson, called his first witness. The witness was Colonel Todaro.

Those in the room watched the door through which the witness would enter. There was an expectant air to the court, like the collective pause of breath at a football game just before the opening kickoff.

Colonel Todaro came in, saluted the board president, was sworn in, then took his seat on the raised platform in the center of the room.

"Colonel Todaro, would you tell the court your position, please?"

"I'm commanding officer of the 86th Attack Helicopter Company, better known as the Gunslingers."

"And Mr. Carmack is one of your pilots?"

"Not just one of my pilots, Major. He is my best pilot."

"What do you mean by that?"

"He has more flying time than anyone in the company, including myself."

"What about combat service time?"

"He's top there, too."

"I see. Tell me, Colonel Todaro, is someone with that much experience likely to become confused and disoriented in the heat of battle? What I mean is, don't we have the reasonable right to expect such a man to —"

"Objection," Reynolds said. "Counsel is leading the witness."

"Sustained," Colonel Sherman said.

Major Patterson stroked his chin and looked at Reynolds. Reynolds was busy, sketching, with considerable skill, the members of the court-martial board.

"Let me reword that question," Major Patterson said. "Have you ever had any reason to doubt Mr. Carmack's performance under pressure?"

"Never."

"Do you have any doubt about his performance under pressure now?"

"None."

"On the fifteenth of November, the day in question, do you think Mr. Carmack cracked under pressure?"

"Objection. Calls for a conclusion," Reynolds said. He didn't even look up from his drawing as he shaded in one of the ribbons on a board officer's chest.

"Sustained."

"Tell me, Colonel Todaro," Major Patterson started, "about the fifteenth of November. What happened on that day?"

"We could have ended the war that day," Todaro began, "if Mr. Carmack hadn't —"

"Objection," Reynolds said.

Before the board president could even react, Major Patterson addressed his witness.

"If you would, sir, just tell what actually happened, as nearly as you can recall, without any personal opinions."

"All right," Todaro said. He ran his hand through his hair. "Our mission orders were to provide lift helicopters for South Vietnamese Special Forces, and gunship cover for the insertion and over the area of operations."

"And did you do that?"

"Yes, sir."

"What about Mr. Carmack?"

"Mr. Carmack was put in command of the Blue

team, a fire team composed of four armed helicopters. His mission was to orbit the area in the event additional firepower would be needed."

"Was it needed?"

"No."

"If it had been needed, would Mr. Carmack have been in position to supply it?"

"No," Todaro said again.

"Why not?"

"Because Mr. Carmack received a request to provide support for a convoy from the 765th Group."

"Did Mr. Carmack answer that request?"

"Yes."

"With your permission?"

"No. I checked with MACV and discovered that in the operational orders for the 765th, any convoy which might require air support would get that support from the nearest available air force or navy air."

"And were either of these elements in position to respond to the call for help?"

"Two Phantom jets from the 507th Fighter Wing in Binh Hoa answered the call."

"I thought you said Mr. Carmack answered the call."

"He did. In fact, he had to move out of the way to let the air force go about its business."

"What happened next?"

"Mr. Carmack returned to the area of operation. Once there, he saw Colonel Mot's men in a mop-up operation and, for some reason known only to him, attacked Colonel Mot, killing him, two

American advisors, and fourteen South Vietnamese soldiers."

"Colonel Todaro, was Colonel Mot known personally to Mr. Carmack?"

"Yes, he was."

"Could he recognize him on sight?"

"Yes, of course."

"But Mr. Carmack was flying a helicopter that day, was he not?"

"That doesn't matter," Todaro said. "Colonel Mot was flying his personal flag. You could see him from the air quite easily."

"Objection," Reynolds said.

This time Major Patterson smiled. "Colonel Todaro, how do you know anyone could see him from the air?"

"I was flying, too," Todaro said. "Colonel Mot's flag stood out like a sore thumb."

"No further questions, Colonel Todaro."

Reynolds laid his pencil across his drawing and looked over at Colonel Todaro.

"Colonel Todaro, would you say the mission on November 15 was successful?"

"To a degree," Todaro answered.

"To what degree?"

"Our hope was that we would be able to break the back of the V.C. once and for all. Colonel Mot had successfully destroyed the V.C. infrastructure the night before, leaving only the soldiers in the field to take care of. We were well on our way to doing that when Colonel Mot was killed."

"I see. And it's your contention that Colonel Mot's death caused the operation to fail?"

"Well, fail its original purpose," Colonel Todaro said. "Though, as I said, it was a successful operation within limits."

"How do you measure this success?"

"Well, by body count," Todaro answered. "There were one hundred seventeen of the enemy killed, while we took only eighteen casualties. Seventeen killed and one wounded."

"Thank you, Colonel Todaro," Reynolds said. "I have no further questions, though I would like to reserve the right to recall this witness."

"Witness is dismissed," said Major Patterson, who, in addition to being the trial counsel, was also the court officer.

Major Patterson's second witness was Sergeant First Class Jack Creech. Creech was a field advisor, assigned to the team that was attached to Colonel Mot's special forces. Creech was the only American who survived the strafing incident.

"Phillips went down first," Creech said. "Then Carmody. Carmody died in my arms."

"Did you make any attempt to notify the helicopters that you were friendly?" Major Patterson asked.

"Hell, yes," Creech said. "I started squawking their parrot from the very first pass."

"I beg your pardon? Squawking their parrot?"

"Yes, sir. That's the IFF. We have a special code and we can punch that into the IFF, and they pick up a squawking noise on their transponder. That's what we call squawking the parrot."

"And you did this?"

"About a hundred times before they finally called

off their attacks. But, by that time, it was too late for Phillips and Carmody."

"What about Colonel Mot? What did he do?"

"When he saw that we couldn't get through on the radio, he moved right out into the open and began waving his flag at them."

"Did the pilots see him?"

"Yes, sir, they seen him," Creech said. He looked over at Carmack. "The leader of the group seemed like he made a special point of zeroing in on the colonel, like as if he wanted to kill him."

"Objection," Reynolds said easily.

"Sustained," Colonel Sherman agreed. "Sergeant Creech, you will answer only such questions as you can answer from personal knowledge. Your opinions are not admissible, and you may find yourself subject to conduct-unbecoming charges, should you persist."

"I'm sorry, sir," Creech answered.

"Sergeant, who was the first person killed in the strafing?" Major Patterson asked.

"I'm not sure. Colonel Mot, he went pretty early."

"Thank you," Major Patterson said. "Your witness."

"Sergeant Creech, what did you think of Colonel Mot?"

"If there was more like him, we'd have this war over with in a hurry," Creech said.

"What makes you say that?"

"Well, say he was in pursuit and the V.C. hauled ass into another sector. The Black Knight didn't bother getting permission from the province chief or ARVN headquarters or anything else. He just went about his job."

"He never checked with the village mayors, or police, or anything?"

"No, sir."

"And you thought that was good?"

"We're supposed to be fightin' a war over here, sir. Colonel Mot told me once that if we made war unpopular enough, there wouldn't be any war."

"I see. Is that the justification he used for attacking villagers? He did attack innocent villagers, didn't he?"

"What the hell do you know about it?" Creech said. "You're a civilian, you don't know shit from Shinola."

"Sergeant Creech?" Colonel Sherman barked angrily. To the surprise of the court, Reynolds held up his hand.

"If it would please the court," he said, "I would like to allow Sergeant Creech the freedom to express what's on his mind."

"Very well," Colonel Sherman said. "Sergeant Creech, you may continue. You are cautioned about the propriety of this court, and the respect due its officers."

"Yes, sir," Creech said.

"Now, Sergeant Creech," Reynolds said. "Would you please explain why you think I don't know shit from Shinola?"

There was nervous laughter from the spectators.

"It ain't just you, sir. It's anyone who hasn't been in the bush. The straphangers and the feather merchants, they think war is soldier against soldier. But I've seen twelve-year-old girls blow a guy away. I've seen pregnant women throw hand grenades, and I've seen old men and old women trigger punji stakes. When you see that, sir, then you know there ain't no such thing as villagers. There's just dinks, and it breaks down to the dinks who are trying to kill you and the dinks who aren't.''

"How do you know the difference?" Reynolds asked.

"You don't always."

"You must have some guidelines."

"Well, sir, when we was with Mot it was simple. If the dink was one of his soldiers, he was one of us . . . if he wasn't one of Mot's soldiers, he was one of them.''

" 'Them' being the bad guys?"

"Yes, sir.''

"What do you do about the bad guys?"

"You kill them. That's what my job was.''

"I see. In the village that Mr. Carmack shot up . . . was it us against them?''

"Yes, sir.''

"So the villagers were the bad guys and Mot's soldiers were the good guys, is that it?''

"Pretty much.''

"Sergeant Creech, were you with Colonel Mot during his raids the night before?''

"Yes, sir.''

"Do you believe he broke the infrastructure of the V.C.?''

"I . . . I can't answer that. I'm only supposed to answer questions I have knowledge about.''

"You had no knowledge about the V.C. infrastructure?''

"Only what Colonel Mot said."

"I see. And did you believe him?"

Creech looked over at the court. "Do I have to answer that question?"

"It's a simple enough question," Reynolds said. "All I want to know is if you, personally, believed Colonel Mot."

"Witness is directed to answer."

Creech sighed. "No, sir," he finally said. "I didn't believe him."

"May I ask why?"

"I speak the language. I heard him talking with some of the officers on his staff. One of them said the Americans wouldn't like him attacking temples like he done, and he said he'd tell them about this infrastructure stuff and everything would be all right."

"Did you tell any of your superiors what you heard?"

"Colonel Mot was my superior."

"Did you tell any of your American superiors?"

"No, sir — that is, no one except Phillips and Carmody. I told them."

"And what did they say or do?"

"Nothing. They said one operation is pretty much like another and it didn't really make any difference."

"Was this like the others, Sergeant Creech? Were you in the habit of rounding up civilians for execution?"

"Objection!" Major Patterson shouted.

"Withdraw the question. How many bad guys were killed, Sergeant Creech?"

"One hundred seventeen."

"And how many weapons were recovered?"

"One."

"One? One hundred seventeen bad guys were killed and only one weapon was recovered? Isn't that unusual?"

"No, sir. You see, the V.C. set great store by their weapons. They'll save a weapon before they'll save one of their own wounded."

"I see. How many casualties did Colonel Mot's force sustain?"

"I don't know."

Reynolds returned to his table and picked up a piece of paper. "Oh, here it is. Eighteen. Seventeen killed and one wounded. Does that sound about right to you? One hundred seventeen of the enemy and eighteen friendlies?"

"Yes, sir. We fought a good fight."

"How about the bad guys? Did they put up much resistance? In fact, was there any resistance at all?"

"We had eighteen casualties," Creech said.

"Did you observe a vigorous return fire?"

"I . . . I don't know."

"You don't know? A moment ago you were deriding the straphangers and feather merchants. You are a man of the bush. Can't you tell if you're getting return fire?"

"Well, sir, we seemed to have things pretty well under control."

"I would say so. Eighteen casualties to one hundred seventeen is a significant difference. In fact, when you stop to realize that the seventeen killed weren't killed by enemy action at all, but by the American helicopters, it becomes even more significant. The eighteenth casualty, the soldier who was wounded, suffered a sprained ankle when he left the helicopter. When you get right down to it, not one casualty was the result of enemy action . . . and yet they lost one hundred seventeen. Who were they, Sergeant Creech? The one hundred seventeen who were killed — were they bad guys?''

"They were V.C."

"V.C. soldiers?"

"V.C.," Creech said again.

"Could they have been villagers?"

"V.C. villagers."

"V.C. villagers who might have been, let's see, what did you say? A twelve-year-old girl, a pregnant woman, an old man, or an old woman — are they the bad guys you killed?''

"I . . . I don't know. Maybe."

"In fact, Sergeant Creech, weren't the entire one hundred seventeen dead comprised of villagers of all ages and sexes, including one infant not yet able to walk?''

"I . . . I don't know. There was so much shooting going on . . . so much confusion. One moment we were in a mopping-up action, and the next we were being attacked by our own helicopters.''

"While Colonel Mot was mopping up?"

"Yes, sir."

"Now, I ask you, Sergeant Creech, is it possible that the mopping up . . . given the fact that some of the bad guys might be twelve-year-old girls, pregnant women, old men, and old women . . . isn't it possible that someone flying over might mistake Colonel Mot's troops, who were dressed in black, as Viet Cong who were murdering villagers?''

"They weren't murdering, sir, they were mopping up," Creech insisted.

"But isn't it possible that from a helicopter one might mistake the mopping-up action for murder?"

"I . . . I guess it's possible, sir," Sergeant Creech said. "I just don't know."

"No further questions."

Colonel Sherman looked at his watch, then cleared his throat.

"At this time, I declare a recess of one hour and thirty minutes. We will begin again at 1300 hours."

# Chapter Sixteen

"If the court please," Reynolds said. "I understand Major Patterson is about to call Song Tay Minh as a witness."

"Have you evidence as to why she shouldn't be called?" Colonel Sherman asked.

"No, sir," Reynolds said. "However, we are prepared to stipulate that Mr. Carmack was sexually intimate with Madam Mot, at the time and place so stated by the young lady. In deference to her age, and to spare her embarrassment, I ask that the court accept our stipulation and dismiss the witness."

"One moment," Colonel Sherman said. The officers of the court huddled for a conference.

"Why don't you let her talk?" Mike asked. "If Mot really was with her, that would show that he knew about Le and me, and that I had no motive, wouldn't it?"

"If Mot knew, the court may decide that you knew he knew. That changes it from a simple foolin' around into what the people in my part of Texas call kinky. We want to portray you as a professional army officer, not as some sex pervert."

"Oh, I see what you mean," Mike said quietly.

The conference of officers broke up and Colonel Sherman cleared his throat.

"The court agrees to accept the stipulation," he said. To Major Patterson, he added, "You may dismiss the witness."

"Court calls Specialist Five Clayton R. Smith."

Smitty, Mike's crew chief, was sworn in. Major Patterson opened his questioning.

"Specialist Smith, did you inform Mr. Carmack of the missing transponder before this mission?"

"Yes, sir," Smitty answered. "And it was written up on the dash-thirteen."

"Isn't that a rather serious problem?"

"It ain't no red-X, sir, if that's what you mean," Smitty said. "You can fly, even without a transponder."

"So when Mr. Carmack began this mission, he knew the transponder was inoperative. He knew he would have no way of verifying an identity code?"

"Yes, sir."

"Despite that, he opened fire against soldiers on the ground, not knowing whether they were friend or foe. Is that correct?"

"He thought they —"

"I'm not interested in what you think he thought. My question is: Did he open fire on those soldiers?"

"Yes, sir," Smitty said quietly.

"No further questions," Patterson said.

"Smitty, as crew chief, do you also man a machine gun?" asked Reynolds.

"Yes, sir. We got two M-60s, one mounted in each cargo door. The door gunner has one, I have the other."

"Did you shoot at any of Colonel Mot's men?"

"Yes, sir, I did," Smitty answered.

"Why?"

"I thought they was V.C.," Smitty answered.

"Objection. Calls for a conclusion," Major Patterson said.

" 'Please the court," Reynolds said. "I was only asking him to justify his own actions . . . not draw a conclusion as to Mr. Carmack's actions."

"Objection denied."

"I have no further questions," Reynolds said.

Major Patterson had no more witnesses, so it was Reynolds's time to bring his witnesses on. His first witness was Captain Mack, commander of the convoy Mike had rescued.

Captain Mack testified that if Mike hadn't arrived when he did, he might have lost his entire convoy. Reynolds's second witness was one of the air force pilots who responded to the call, Major Clifton Hazzard. Major Hazzard stated that when he arrived on the scene the helicopters had already stemmed the V.C. attack, and all he provided was mop-up services. Both officers agreed that Mike's response to the call saved the lives of two dozen American soldiers.

Reynolds's final witness was Ernie Chapel.

"Mr. Chapel, what is your position?"

"I'm a reporter for Combined Press International," Ernie said.

"You're here to cover the war for the folks back home, are you?"

"For the people back home, for anyone who wants to know."

"Mr. Chapel, how long have you been in Vietnam?"

"Five years," Ernie answered.

"Five years? You were here when Diem was killed?"

"Yes, I was."

"Tell us a little about your combat experience," Reynolds invited.

"Understand, none of it is actually combat experience; I have always been an observer," Ernie said.

"Tell us about some of the combat you've observed," Reynolds suggested.

"During World War Two, I went ashore with the marines on Iwo Jima and Okinawa. I rode in some of the B-29s during the fire-bomb raids over Tokyo. During the Korean War I went ashore for the Inchon landing, made the long, cold march down from the Chosin Reservoir, followed the troops up Pork Chop Hill. In Vietnam, I participated in Operation Junction City, Rolling Thunder, and half a dozen other operations over the last five years. I hitched a ride on a Phantom jet for a mission over Hanoi, and a Skyraider for a dive-bombing and strafing attack outside Da Nang.''

"And you've flown in helicopters before?"

"Several times, yes, sir."

Reynolds turned to the court. "Unless there is some challenge to Mr. Chapel's level of experience, I would now like to present him as an expert witness."

"Expert in what field, sir?" Major Patterson asked, puzzled by Reynolds's strategy.

"Expert in the observation and evaluation of men under fire. His unique position as a war correspondent has given him a ringside seat to three wars. Is there anyone present in this court who can match his experience?"

"Court agrees to regard Mr. Chapel as an expert witness," Colonel Sherman said.

"Thank you. Mr. Chapel, as an expert witness, I ask you to evaluate Mr. Carmack's performance on the fifteenth of June."

"Objection!" Patterson boomed. "Colonel, surely we aren't going to be subjected to the distant observation of a reporter, no matter how experienced he is!"

"Please allow me to qualify this," Reynolds said, holding up a finger. "I'm not asking for a general evaluation. I'm asking for a specific report based on direct observation. You were in the helicopter with Mr. Carmack, were you not?"

"Yes, I was," Ernie said.

There was a collective gasp in the courtroom. Then Colonel Sherman looked sharply at Major Patterson.

"Major Patterson, were you aware Mr. Chapel was in that helicopter?"

"His name wasn't on the dash-twelve," Major Patterson said.

"I've been informed that only flight crew are listed on the dash-twelve. But I do have signed statements and certificates from the enlisted and officers of Mr. Carmack's fire team to verify that Chapel was aboard," said Reynolds. "Will you accept that?"

"Do I have to?" Patterson looked at Colonel Sherman.

"For the sake of expediency, perhaps you'd better," said Sherman.

"Very well," said Patterson, begrudgingly.

"Proceed," Sherman said.

"Did you see Colonel Mot's troops on the ground?" Reynolds asked.

"I saw troops on the ground, dressed in black, shooting villagers," Ernie said.

"Shooting at villagers?" Colonel Sherman asked.

"No, sir," Ernie said. "They were shooting villagers. They were lining them up — men, women, and children — and they were shooting them."

"What did you think?"

"I thought what all of us thought," Ernie answered. "I thought the men in black were V.C."

"Did Mr. Carmack attempt to contact the troops on the ground to determine if they were friend or foe?"

"Yes, sir."

"How could he do that without a transponder?"

"He asked one of the other pilots to contact

them. The other pilot came back on the radio and said there was no response."

"Then what happened?"

"We made two strafing attacks. When we were starting our third, the pilot came on and said that his parrot had squawked, and he had received a message on the FM frequency saying the soldiers on the ground were friendly."

"What did Mr. Carmack do then?"

"He terminated the attack."

"At the beginning of the questioning, I asked you to evaluate Mr. Carmack's performance on that day. Would you do that for us, please?"

"I consider Mr. Carmack one of the most capable and dependable officers I have ever encountered. On the day in question, he was calm and collected. He made every effort to identify the troops on the ground and, not getting any response, acted on what I considered to be the reasonable assumption that black-clad soldiers who were shooting civilian women and children were not friendly."

"Did you know Colonel Mot?"

"Yes, sir."

"How well?"

"I had been his guest a couple of times. We were speaking acquaintances."

"But you didn't recognize him from the air?"

"No, sir."

"Colonel Todaro claimed that he was able to pick out Colonel Mot from the air by his flag. In fact, several other pilots said the same thing. Couldn't you have done that?"

"He may have been flying his personal flag

earlier, when we were absent from the area. It wasn't flying when we made the attack.''

"We heard testimony that Colonel Mot waved his flag in an attempt to stop the attack.''

"If he did, I didn't see it," Ernie said. "And no one on board any of the helicopters saw it.''

"In your expert opinion, was Mr. Carmack justified in making his attack on Colonel Mot?''

"In that he didn't know it was Colonel Mot, and the troops were murdering villagers, Mr. Carmack was not only right to make the attack . . . it would have been criminal to allow the massacre to continue.''

"Objection. Calls for a conclusion," said Major Patterson.

"Sustained.''

"Thank you, Mr. Chapel.''

"Mr. Chapel," Patterson started. "You say that you might have known the troops were friendly had you been there earlier to see Colonel Mot's flag. Why weren't you there?''

"We were answering a call for assistance from a convoy under attack.''

"Against orders?''

"Beg pardon?''

"Didn't Colonel Todaro issue specific orders not to answer the call?''

"Yes.''

"But Mr. Carmack, the officer you just characterized as capable and dependable, disobeyed those orders. Why?''

"By the time Mr. Carmack's request to render assistance was answered, we were already over the target area. Mr. Carmack had information that

Colonel Todaro didn't have, because we were in a position to see that the V.C. were about to overrun the convoy. Based on that information, Mr. Carmack exercised sound judgment and leadership.''

"Nevertheless, he did disobey orders, did he not?''

"Yes, but —''

"Yes or no?''

"Yes.''

"Thank you. No further questions.''

"Defense recalls Colonel Todaro.''

Colonel Todaro took the stand a second time. Then Reynolds walked over to question him.

"Colonel, given the circumstances as you now know them, would you still have ordered Mr. Carmack not to render assistance to the convoy?''

"As I now know them . . . I would have allowed Mr. Carmack to answer the call,'' Todaro agreed reluctantly.

"Thank you, Colonel.''

"But that still doesn't —''

"Thank you, Colonel,'' Reynolds said again.

"Witness may step down,'' Colonel Sherman said.

During his summation, Major Patterson tried to point out motive, opportunity, and premeditation. The motive, he said, was confirmed by Mr. Carmack's admission that he was having an affair with Madam Mot. The opportunity was evident by the fact that he found himself in a helicopter over a confused field of battle, and used that confusion to commit murder.

"Premeditation, I admit, is more difficult to

prove, for how can you look into a man's mind to measure the intention of his soul? However, the fact that Madam Mot committed suicide shortly after Mr. Carmack was charged indicates to me that she knew the trail of evidence would lead right to her. It could only lead to her if she was guilty . . . and as she was not in the helicopter, she could only be guilty of conspiracy. Conspiracy, by definition, means premeditation. Therefore, I ask you to find Mr. Carmack guilty of Article 118 of the UCMJ. Murder.''

Greyhound Reynolds stood up and looked at the court, letting his eyes move across the face of every officer present. Overhead a helicopter that was returning from a flight beat through the air, its blades popping loudly as the pilot descended through his own rotor wash. In the windows three air conditioners hummed softly. Reynolds waited for a long moment. Finally he began to talk. His voice was so low the board had to strain to hear him.

"The question you are asked to decide is a simple one," he said. "Did Mr. Carmack kill Colonel Mot because of some crazed action to rid the world of the man so he would be free to pursue his relationship with Madam Mot? Or was this an accident, brought on by Colonel Mot's own bloodlust?

"Consider this," he went on. "Mr. Carmack attempted, through other pilots in his flight, to identify the soldiers who were engaged in the brutal massacre of innocent villagers. There were three other helicopters in the flight, and all three were trying to raise a signal on their transponder. Not one did.

"Consider this as well. Every helicopter in the flight fired at the soldiers. Admittedly, some of them were new, but there was in every helicopter at least one officer and one enlisted man with previous combat experience. And," Reynolds said, holding up his finger, "there was riding, as a passenger in Mr. Carmack's helicopter, Mr. Ernie Chapel, who, by the certification of this very court, is recognized as an expert in combat observation. Despite all this there was not one man . . . not one . . . who refused to fire. Why? Because to a man they thought they were firing at V.C. to save innocent villagers.

"When, at last, one of the pilots did pick up the identifying code, the attack was terminated immediately.

"Now, that brings up a question which has not been addressed by this court. Why was Colonel Mot butchering innocent men, women, and children? Perhaps it is not the function of this court to answer that question . . . but I believe it is the duty of this court to raise another. Is it possible that there may be certain elements in the South Vietnamese Army who don't want this question asked? Could these be the same people who insisted that the Americans charge Mr. Carmack with Mot's murder?

"Gentlemen, I am not interested in why Colonel Mot was murdering villagers. Perhaps it is a question of international politics. I am perfectly willing to leave the question begging. I am, however, interested in the fate of Mike Carmack. I cannot believe, and . . . *I will not allow* . . . an officer who has performed such valuable, loyal, and courageous service to be the sarcrificial lamb no matter what the political reason.''

Reynolds walked back over to his table and stood there for a long moment, letting the power of his last few words sink in. Finally, with a courtly nod, he sat down.

''The defense rests,'' he said quietly.

# Epilogue

**WASHINGTON
SPRING, 1986**

Mike Carmack was found innocent, though he didn't get away without cost. The army remembered it, and when the big reduction in force came about in 1972, CW-3 Mike Carmack, who had eighteen years in the army, lost his retirement benefits when he was removed from the active-duty rolls. It was a matter of fiscal responsibility, the army said, and not only Mike, but also several thousand other warrant and commissioned officers were released.

Ernie saw Mike about ten years later, down in Mexico. He had been flying helicopters for some high-risk oil exploration company, and when the company went bankrupt, Mike was stranded with no money and nowhere to go. Ernie tried to loan him money, but Mike would never take it.

Then, just six months later, Ernie got a letter from him. In it was a picture of Mike and one of the most beautiful women Ernie had ever seen.

Can you believe Colonel Todaro has a daughter like this? Hard to figure, isn't it? Never in a thousand years would I have thought Todaro would wind up as my father-in-law, but that he is. I met her in Hollywood.

That's what I said . . . Hollywood. Maria works as a secretary for Helicopter Action Sequences, the company that hired me. I've got a cushy job flyin' for the movies. Shit, a flight with only one-half the pucker factor we used to pull in Nam now pays five to ten thousand. Why the hell didn't I do this a long time ago? By the way . . . I never collected that dinner you beat me out of at the My Kahn . . .

The shadows grew long at the Vietnam monument, and the line thinned. Ernie stepped up to the black polished stone and raised his hand to the chiseled letters. He let his fingers slide across the ridges of John Rindell's name.

"I retired today, John," Ernie said quietly. "They wanted to give me a dinner . . . told me the White House press secretary would come. They couldn't believe I turned them down, didn't know why I didn't want to celebrate.

"They just don't understand, that's all. I'm going to celebrate. I'm going to have that dinner we never had at the My Kahn . . . drink a few cold beers to make up for all the hot ones we had to drink over there. And then, if I'm lucky, I might even find a woman to talk to who doesn't think my hair is too white, my face too wrinkled, or my eyes too old.

"How 'bout it, John? You wanna come along?"

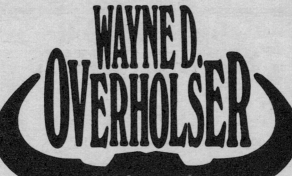

# WAYNE D. OVERHOLSER

## WESTERNS

**WHITEWATER POLICE**

## JOHN BALL
AUTHOR OF **IN THE HEAT OF THE NIGHT** INTRODUCING, **POLICE CHIEF JACK TALLON** IN THESE EXCITING, FAST-PACED MYSTERIES.

# FREE!!
# BOOKS BY MAIL
# CATALOGUE

BOOKS BY MAIL will share with you our current bestselling books as well as hard to find specialty titles in areas that will match your interests. You will be updated on what's new in books at no cost to you. Just fill in the coupon below and discover the convenience of having books delivered to your home.

*PLEASE ADD $1.00 TO COVER THE COST OF POSTAGE & HANDLING.*

## BOOKS BY MAIL

**320 Steelcase Road E.,**
**Markham, Ontario L3R 2M1**

**210 5th Ave., 7th Floor**
**New York, N.Y., 10010**

Please send Books By Mail catalogue to:

Name _____
        (please print)

Address _____

City _____

Prov./State _____ P.C./Zip _____

(BBM1)